Runaway Raft

Other Books by
RUTH HARNDEN

Golly and the Gulls
The High Pasture
Summer's Turning

Runaway Raft

RUTH HARNDEN

Illustrated by Marvin Friedman

1968 HOUGHTON MIFFLIN COMPANY BOSTON

For Mary K.

1

BART WENT UP and down the hall a number of times doing his best to distract his older brother who was talking on the telephone. Finally he went into the kitchen and asked his mother if she couldn't make Alec get off the phone. "He's been talking for *hours*," he told her.

His mother looked mildly sympathetic, but she only said, "Don't exaggerate, dear. You'll just have to be a little patient and wait for your turn. Then you can talk just as long — "

"I don't want a *turn!*" Bart broke in. "That isn't the point at all. It's just that — well suppose someone wanted to call here? Someone might, you know. And all he's doing, anyway, is talking to that Liz that he probably saw about ten minutes ago."

"Well," his mother said reasonably, "if he saw her ten minutes ago he can't have been talking very long."

"Three minutes!" Bart said. "That's what a telephone call is supposed to be. *Three* minutes. Oh!" he said in helpless frustration, "what's the use?" and he stormed out of the room.

1

He went back down the hall again, making as much noise as possible, and he glared at his brother again while he was about it. Alec saw him, too. He looked right back at Bart, though he didn't even change the expression on his face, which was pretty silly in Bart's opinion. You'd think he'd at least be embarrassed, Bart was thinking. Gosh! His brother was about the most superior character in the world all the rest of the time. Bossing everybody around! He acted as if somebody had put him in charge of the universe. And you'd think everyone was feebleminded except him, the way he treated people. But *he* was the one that really looked like an idiot the minute he started talking to that Liz. Nobody would even recognize him.

Back in his own room Bart got out the list of customers on his new paper route, and started going through it. He wanted to really memorize it and not have to take it along with him again, even tomorrow. It was a great route! Oh, he knew it wasn't the easiest, like just going from house to house up and down the streets right here in town. They probably gave the easy ones to the older kids who'd sort of proved themselves, and kept the tough ones for the beginners, like himself. But it suited Bart just fine! First he had to ride his bike about a mile out of town. Even that part was pretty, and interesting. But when he got to the river, that was the greatest!

He'd always loved the Salt River, as long as he could remember, and someday he intended to explore it. It was a tidal river, and when the tide was going out or

2

coming in the water moved very fast. It was considered to be a little dangerous, too, especially way down at the mouth of the river where it swept out into the sea. Bart's father thought it was more than a little dangerous, and when Bart talked about getting a canoe, or a skiff, his father always said firmly: "Not for the Salt River." So Bart had had to content himself with simply dreaming about it.

What he'd been dreaming about for some time now was a raft. He figured he could build it himself, and it wouldn't cost him any more than the price of the lumber. It ought to be pretty safe, too; not tippy like a boat, but broad, and solid, and low. Right down flat on the water. How could anything upset that?

By raft was the way Bart really wanted to know the Salt River. But, in the meantime, he was at least going to get acquainted with its shores, and learn something about its course. Already, just today, he knew a lot more than he'd ever known before. He had a very good idea of the river's considerable length, and he knew how it wound, and curved, sometimes through trees but more often through broad, bright meadows of marsh grass.

The houses which were on his route were all new to him, since they were all situated along the water and couldn't be seen from the road. Some of them were pretty big, and impressive, with clipped lawns sloping down to the river. And some of them were very small and simple, and built rather close to the water. Because the river was so winding, hardly any one of the houses was in sight of any other. This gave to each one of them, however small, a particular spaciousness, an air of great peace and privacy as though the whole river belonged to that house alone. And every one of them had at least one boat, moored to a small dock, or rocking gently at the end of a rope that was fastened to the nearest tree. There wasn't a single house that Bart wouldn't have moved into in a minute if he could have had his way. And he bet that even his father wouldn't try to keep him off the Salt River if it ran through their own front yard.

He made himself concentrate on his list. It wasn't really so awfully long. It was just that the houses were so spaced out that the actual route was pretty long. Brown — he seemed to remember that as a big, white house with sheds and a barn at the back, like an old farm. Matson — he thought that was where he'd seen all those cats and kittens. Carter — Heck! He was sure that was the place where they had the big dog. It was a Doberman. And since the dog was strange to him and he was certainly a stranger to the dog, he'd tossed the paper over the hedge and beat it back to his bike. At the time it had seemed to him the only thing to do, but he didn't feel right about it just the same. He wasn't at all sure where the paper had landed. It might be under a bush somewhere, or buried in a flower bed, and maybe the people would never find it. The anxiety that had sent him up and down the hall such a short time ago was gnawing at him again.

A minute later Alec pushed open his door, without

4

even having knocked. If Bart ever did that to Alec he'd get his head taken off. But any old time Alec wanted to borrow something, or make a criticism, or start an argument he just busted in. "What's the idea?" he demanded now, "stamping around the house and making faces like a madman when a person's trying to carry on a quiet, civilized conversation?"

Bart gathered all his strength and said, "Why don't you try carrying on a quiet, civilized conversation with your own family once in a while? Nobody's hard of hearing, you know."

"I *said*," Alec told him, speaking even more loudly and distinctly, "what's the idea?"

Bart hung onto himself. "I was trying to get you off the phone," he said. "It seems to me that anyone with half a brain — never mind being a genius — could figure that out."

Alec suddenly relaxed and leaned his weight against the doorjamb. His most superior look was taking over his face. "No kidding," he said. "You mean *you* wanted the phone? Well, well, the baby's growing up."

Bart gritted his teeth. "I've got a job," he said, "and that's a lot more important than — "

"You mean that little old *paper* route?" his brother broke in.

"It's a darned good route! It's a better route than you ever had, I bet." Bart's voice had shaken a little in spite of himself.

"O.K., O.K.," Alec said. "But you don't have to suddenly act as if you're running for congress or something."

"But this was my first day," Bart protested.

"So?"

"I just thought," Bart said stubbornly, "somebody might want to call up and make a complaint, for instance."

His brother simply stared at him for a second. "You've got to be kidding," he said then.

Bart folded up his list and stuffed it into a pocket. "I don't see why you say that," he said. "Just because you don't take anything seriously — except yourself."

"Listen," Alex said in a tone of exaggerated patience, "there's a big difference between taking things seriously and being a madman or a worrywart. What are you, anyway, a glutton for punishment?"

Almost the worst thing about Alec was that he could sometimes reduce Bart to tears. Bart was feeling close to them right now. In desperation he said defiantly, "I like to worry!"

After a surprised second Alec laughed. "I guess that's right," he said. He made a corkscrew motion with one finger against his own temple. Bart thought it was pretty feeble, and he guessed his brother did, too, because right after that Alec eased himself out of the room.

"Hey!" Bart called after him. "Close the door, why don't you?" A minute later Bart got up and closed it himself. It was the only way he could get any peace. If Alec wasn't bullying him, Bart could still hear him all over the house, giving some argument to his mother, or

7

really getting into it with his father. It seemed to Bart that Alec upset his father at least as much as he upset Bart. There didn't seem to be much of anything those two could agree about, and sometimes his father shouted just as loud as Alec. Only his mother managed somehow to keep calm, most of the time anyway.

Poor Mom! Bart thought briefly. She was always caught in the middle, and she certainly did her best to keep the peace. One day Bart had overheard her talking to his father, trying to explain Alec — as if anybody could do that! "He's just got a severe case of adolescence," she was saying. "He'll outlive it." Bart's father said, "I just hope I will."

Bart sighed and went back to his own dream. He was going to save every cent he made! And if he did a really great job, maybe he'd get a raise. Then he'd buy the lumber and start building his raft. Of course that part was going to be kind of a problem. Where could he work on it without anyone knowing about it? And then they'd guess what he had in mind — about pushing off, and maybe for good. Sometimes, when things were at their worst, he really thought he'd go forever. He might find an island, for instance, where no one could bother him and he could live just the way he liked. Of course his mother would probably kind of miss him. That made him feel bad for a minute. But right away he told him-self that he could probably work out some way to get in touch with her now and again. Anyway, even if he

8

didn't actually go forever, right away, it would certainly be great to know that he *could.*

He fished out his list again. "Hey!" he said suddenly. He'd just had a brilliant idea. Maybe he could make friends with some of those people along the Salt River, and then they'd let him build his raft right there. It was perfect! It was so perfect it made him laugh out loud, all by himself. Gosh! He hadn't even *asked* for that route. It was just given to him! And here it was, *exactly* what he needed for his plan. It was all so perfect that it practically made him feel superstitious — as if it was absolutely meant to be.

2

Just before setting out on his paper route the next afternoon, Bart decided to collect something for a treat for that Doberman. Treat? More like a bribe, he told himself truthfully. He thought a bone would be just the thing, so he checked the refrigerator, and then the whole kitchen. The only bone in the house seemed to be in a kettle of soup simmering at the back of the stove. Bart examined it anyway, just in case it didn't amount to much and might possibly be removed without being missed. No use, though. He quickly concluded that its absence might cause him even more trouble than the dog could. It was a ham bone, pretty good sized and with a lot of meat on it still. His mother liked to make pea soup with the remains of a ham in it. It was great, too. No one appreciated it more than Bart himself, and he knew perfectly well that he might as well steal the whole kettle of soup as to try sneaking the bone out of it.

He wracked around the kitchen some more and then he started in on the pantry shelves. In the end he settled

10

for stuffing his pockets with cookies. They might not be as good as dog biscuits. On the other hand, with any luck the Doberman might like them even better. If they didn't work, Bart promised himself that tomorrow he'd go to the market and make a real investment. He might buy half a pound of hamburg, for instance. Suppose it cost thirty-five cents? Suppose it was as much as forty, he thought recklessly. Ater all it would be worth it if it did the trick. His whole plant — his whole future, really — depended on keeping his job.

It was the first warm day of spring. Bart hadn't been pedaling for very long when he had to stop and take off his jacket. While he bundled it up and crammed it into his bike basket on top of the papers he'd folded already, he noticed how nice the air smelled. It wasn't exactly fragrant, the way it would be any day now when the apple trees began to blossom, and the daffodils opened in people's yards. It was more like the smell of freshly turned earth, and made him think about flowers. It was a promising sort of smell.

Starting on again, feeling cooler, he began to think about another smell that would meet him very soon now — the smell of the Salt River, and the sea beyond. When the wind blew east he could smell it from his own backyard — a keen, briny smell that made him feel restless and deeply satisfied, together. It wasn't like anything else in the world. Trying to think one time just how it affected him, he had decided it was like being hungry and being full all at the same time.

11

Bart even liked the low-tide smell, which was entirely different. There was nothing stirring or challenging about that. It was just a clammy old mud-flat smell. His father called it "primordial" and he said people probably liked it because all life had originally come out of the primordial slime, and the liking was a kind of remembering way beyond conscious memory. The idea briefly fascinated Bart. But really he was more interested in the future than in the past.

At the ancient stone bridge that spanned the river he stopped and got off his bike for a real look at the water. At either end of its arch the bridge was low enough to see over. Bart put his elbows on the flattest stones and, by leaning over, he was able to see straight down. The tide looked to be almost full, but it hadn't turned yet. The water was flowing, almost racing, inland from the sea.

There was no question of seeing the bottom. The river was much too deep for that. Many years ago, as he knew, ships had been built along this river, and then sailed down it to the sea. Some of those ships had sailed around the world, so they must have been really good sized. That meant they drew a lot of water. They couldn't possibly have navigated any ordinary inland river.

For a number of minutes Bart watched the swift water and the long grasses, just below the surface, being pulled by the current the way hair might be pulled by a comb. When the tide turned, the grasses would all start stream-

12

ing in the opposite direction. He kept thinking that was going to happen any minute and he'd like to wait and see it. For one thing, he'd like to know if the grass ever got uprooted in the tug of the tide's reversal. The grass looked very delicate, and the tide was obviously very strong. And how could anything be so firmly embedded in that watery bottom? He wondered about all that, but the grasses went on streaming inland, and the tide still didn't turn. Reluctantly Bart got off his elbows and went back to his bike.

Shortly beyond the bridge the narrow road that was his route forked off sharply from the main, paved road. It had perhaps originally been a towpath that followed the river. It was still unpaved, but had been given a surface of tar sprinkled with sand that was firm enough for bicycling. For a bit it paralleled the river, but then usage, or the crowding growth of shrubbery and trees, sent it farther in from the shore, and presently the water was no longer in sight. Now there was nothing to be seen but the bushes at either side misted with the green of their earliest, tiny leaves. At places the branches met overhead, and it was like riding through a long green tunnel.

The green tunnel came out into a broad, sunny field with a view of the river again. Halfway down the field that sloped to the water was the rambling farmhouse of Bart's first customer. He said "Brown" to himself, and a minute later got off his bike and took the top paper out of his basket. There didn't seem to be anyone around,

13

and there was no car in the barn that apparently served as a garage. The wide doors stood open and he could see a pile of old tires in what he figured was meant to be a horse stall. The back wall of the barn was almost covered with tacked-up license plates. It struck him as a funny thing to save, but it looked as if they'd saved every license plate they'd ever had. He decided to stick the paper into the crossbeam on the open door. They'd have to see it the minute they drove in, and still it was sort of an unusual place to put it. Maybe it would make them think about him, the way he was thinking about them. What were they like? Would they make friends with him? Would this turn out to be the place where he could build his raft? Before starting back to the road, where he'd propped up his bike, he looked down the slope to the river. There was an old catboat beached near the pier, probably waiting to be scraped and painted which it certainly needed. Maybe he should offer to help them with it. He could come back on Saturday, for instance. That would be a great way to get acquainted. First, they'd probably think he was looking for a job and expected to be paid for what he did. But *Heck,* he said, beginning to imagine the conversation, *I've got a job! I'd just like to help you. I mean I'd really enjoy it. To tell you the truth,* he might throw in, *I'm keen about this river.* That's all he'd say to start with. He wouldn't say anything about his plan and all, just at first. It made him smile to think about it. Before turning away he really cased the yard, if you could call it a yard. It was a great big, huge old field between the house and the river. And it didn't look swampy, either. That catboat was dry as a bone, and just leaning on the grass as if it were on solid ground.

"Hey!" he called out suddenly, because up there on the road there was a kid fooling with his bike. The kid stopped spinning the front wheel, and looked up. He was bigger than Bart, but even at this distance Bart was pretty sure he wasn't any older. Closer to, he was sure of it. The kid squinted his eyes, studying Bart, as if he couldn't see too well, or else he was trying to look tough.

"Why don't you oil this piece of junk once in a while?" he demanded when Bart had come up beside him.

Bart still thought of his bike as the next thing to new. It was only a year old, and while he didn't polish it and oil it all the time the way he used to when he first got it, he didn't exactly neglect it, either. But now he had to look at it again, and he really examined it. That was the kind of thing people could do to you if they were mean enough. They could really shake your confidence in just about anything. The bike looked all right, just as he'd thought it did. In fact it looked practically great, as far as he was concerned. "I didn't notice you had any trouble spinning that wheel," he said with more confidence.

The kid just shrugged. "You get it in really good shape," he said, "and I might give you a few bucks for it. Or — tell you what — I might trade."

Bart shook his head. "Nothing doing," he said.

15

"I've got a Raleigh," the kid told him. "With gears."

Normally Bart would have said something nice, or asked him about the gears and how he liked them. He was curious, as a matter of fact. He'd have liked to know how much difference gears could actually make on a long hill, for example. But he really didn't like this kid. Furthermore, he didn't believe him. So he said, "Yeah, I just bet!" and turned away to get on his bike again and leave.

In the next minute he had the kid's full, grappling weight on his back. It very nearly threw him off balance. But in a way it didn't surprise him. He even had time to think, in a brief flash, that this was exactly what he might have expected. He was just the kind of guy who would wait until your back was turned and then jump you. More than anything else, though, he was aware of the kid's weight. He was only a little taller than Bart, but he was a lot heftier. It was almost like being tackled by a grown man. But this was something that Bart had learned how to deal with.

Luckily both his hands were free. He flung his arms up and back and gripped the back of the kid's neck in his tensed hands. A minute later he had thrown the kid over his head and stretched him out flat on his back on the ground. Bart was breathing a little hard, but the other kid acted as if the wind had been knocked clean out of him. Bart stood looking down at him until he began to recover and then was able to get to his feet. From astonishment the look on his face had changed to
16

one of considerable respect. "Will you teach me that trick?" he asked.

Bart just said, "No," and moved toward his bike again.

The kid was looking at him curiously now. "I don't get you," he said. "Are you a friend or an enemy?" Bart felt like saying "Neither," but the kid was going right on. "You could have really beat up on me just now when I was down and out. So how come you want to be so mean about that trick? What d'you call it — judo? Where'd you learn it, anyway?"

"From my brother." It was one thing he could really thank Alec for. This was the first time he'd actually had to use it, but it had worked like a charm. Alec had really schooled him. Right now he was feeling so grateful that he almost liked his brother.

"What'll you take for teaching me?" the kid asked then.

Holding one handlebar, Bart stretched out a foot to release the stand that propped up his bike. "That's something else I don't like about you," he said slowly. "You seem to think you can buy anything you want. Well you can't! Some things aren't for sale."

"What do you mean by something *else* you don't like?" the kid wanted to know.

"It would take me a long time to tell you," Bart said, "and I've got to get on with my paper route."

"O.K.," the kid said, speaking fast. "Just show me how to do that trick — "

Bart threw one leg over his bike. "In the first place," he said, "it wouldn't do you any good. You wouldn't have any use for it. It's just a way for a person to *defend* himself — against guys like you. All *you* want to do is go around attacking people. Especially when they aren't looking!" He was about to ride off when he noticed that the kid was narrowing his eyes again.

"Suppose I jumped you right now," he said. "Head on, and all. You got a trick for that, too?"

18

Bart considered his own position, straddling the bike the way he was, and balancing on his toes. Just the same he said, "Yup!" He knew he was taking a certain chance, but he was betting the guy wasn't about to risk another trouncing. The more he studied him, in fact, the more convinced he felt about that narrow-eyed look. It was meant to look tough, but what the kid actually looked was wary. Bart thought of his father saying a bully was always a coward. He'd never been so sure that his father was right.

He'd have liked to think of some brilliant parting shot, but all he could do was shove off. Probably some inspiration would occur to him about an hour from now, or tomorrow morning. Still — he'd come off all right. More than all right, really. He began to feel good. He decided he might even tell Alec about it — if his brother was being halfway human, for a change, and like someone you could communicate with.

Pedaling along, with the cool salty wind in his face, he started imagining the conversation. He imagined Alec being pretty impressed. Well — interested, anyway, he thought more sensibly. Just getting Alec's attention and having him really listen would be quite an achievement. Like practically impossible, Bart told himself next. The pleasant image of Alec hanging on his every word began to fade from his mind. It was pure dreaming. If Bart expected anyone to say, "No kidding! And you mean he was way bigger than you and heavy as an ox? Well, go on! What happened then?

What did you do after that?" — if he expected anyone to say things like that it would have to be someone besides his brother. If Alec said anything at all it would be more like, "What did you have to worry about? I taught you, didn't I?" Bart sighed. He guessed he was a hopeless optimist. And that was pretty weird when he stopped to think about it since most of the time he was a hopeless worrywart. Maybe he was crazy?

Almost at once he quit worrying about that because, around a bend in the road, he came in sight of someone who struck him as looking really crazy.

3

Bart's second customer was Matson, just as he had remembered. Up by the road there was a postbox with the name lettered on it in red paint. His memory of the house was accurate, too. It was small, not much bigger than a cabin, and it was situated way down the slope, close to the river. A footpath went from the road down to the house, and right now someone was walking up the path. The person was wearing pants or slacks, but the big floppy-brimmed yellow hat couldn't belong to anyone but a woman.

But what had struck Bart as looking so strange was that the woman had a tiny black kitten riding on top of her hat. Furthermore a big black cat was stretched across her shoulders. Just at first Bart had thought she was wearing a fur piece, but then he saw the cat's tail wave. A couple of tiger cats were walking ahead of her, and half a dozen assorted types trotted at her heels.

His impulse was to get to the postbox and leave her paper before she reached the road. But he didn't ex-

21

actly want to speed up and then rush off again right in front of her. He tried to tell himself that maybe she wasn't really crazy. Maybe she was just crazy about cats, though it was something he couldn't personally imagine. She was walking slowly, and a little unevenly. Probably she was very old. Or else she was trying to balance the kitten on her head without letting it fall off.

By the time he'd got to her box and then unearthed her paper, she was near enough for him to see that she wasn't really old. She mightn't be much older than his mother. And she certainly didn't look as if there was much of anything wrong with her. In fact she had a very sensible sort of face. Plain and sensible, and like someone who was outdoors a lot of the time. She looked permanently tan, the way sailors and boatmen generally looked in Bart's experience. He began to feel a hopeful interest in her, and when she called out, "You the new paper boy?" he called back that he was, and proceeded to wait for her. After all, she was the first person he'd actually encountered who lived along the river.

When she'd come up close she said, "Would you like a kitten?" and reached up for the one on her head. It took both her hands to detach the kitten's claws from her hat and keep the hat on her head. "Though frankly," she told him, "I'd rather you took a cat. They're always harder to place."

"I don't know — " Bart said cautiously. "I don't know much about cats."

22

23

"Lots of people think they do when they don't," she said. "At least you'd be starting with an open mind."

Bart didn't have any intention of starting at all so he just said, "How come you want to give them away — or sell them, or whatever?"

"I'm not trying to sell them," she said promptly. "Though some people in this world don't properly value anything unless it costs money." Bart nodded sympathetically. "I've got too many," she said. "Can't let 'em go homeless, and starve, so I take 'em in — "

"How many have you got?" he asked.

She laughed briefly. "Last I knew there were fourteen. Then two of the mother cats had litters at the same time. That's when I quit counting. This little fellow belongs to still another litter — five in that batch, and no two of them look alike."

"Do they always follow you around?" Bart wanted to know.

"Mostly when they're hungry," she told him. " 'Bout time for their suppers right now."

Bart said, "Gosh! What do you feed them all?"

"Fish, liver, kibbles — they like variety — "

"Do you catch the fish?" Bart broke in, seizing the opportunity to get the conversation closer to his own interest.

"Have to," she said, "if I don't want to go broke. Got to buy everything else."

"I guess that's pretty convenient," he suggested,

"where you're right on the river, and all. Do you go out in a boat, or do you fish off your pier?"

"Both," she told him. "At different times. Depends on the tide, and the weather, of course."

"Does it really get dangerous?" he asked her. "I mean, that's what my father thinks. Whenever I talk about wanting a boat — and I guess I've mentioned it quite a few times — he always starts in on the Salt River and how dangerous it is."

She was looking at him thoughtfully. "Parents!" she said then. "They worry too much."

Bart was secretly pleased with her attitude, but he confessed that he did quite a bit of worrying himself. "Only I worry about different things," he said.

At that she laughed. "You a good swimmer?" she asked.

"I won a medal last summer at day camp," he told her. "After that they said I could take up sailing. But it was almost the end of the summer so I only got out once."

"Shucks!" she said. "I could teach you to sail."

Bart had only one thing to say about that. "When?"

"Well, let's see — " she seemed to be considering it. Maybe she hadn't really meant that she'd actually do it. Or maybe she was going to change her mind. Bart was beginning to really worry by the time she got around to saying, "Spring's a whimsical season. You can get unaccountable high tides. Worse than that, though, the winds are likely to be shifty and undependable. You

25

can capsize in a second, or you can be in irons — "

"Irons?" Bart said, trying to imagine what that might mean.

"Hmm," she said. "There you are. You know anything about navigation? Ever see a chart of this harbor?" Bart shook his head. "Know one buoy from another? Would you know what I meant if I said 'red right returning'?" Bart could only keep helplessly shaking his head. "Good!" she said unexpectedly then. "We'll start there. By the time you've got some notion of how to get in and out of a harbor it should be about time to get out the sails. Meantime, if you'd care to, you can help me paint the hull."

"Sure!" Bart said. "I mean I'd be glad to." The extent of his ignorance had really embarrassed him, so he had to say now, "I'm pretty good at painting, anyway."

She smiled. "Sounds as if you've had some experience." Bart nodded. "So it's a bargain," she said. "What's your name, by the way?" When he'd told her she said, "People call me Matty," and put out her hand to shake Bart's. "Would you like to start Saturday?"

Bart said he certainly would. "Only — does it matter when? My father generally has some chores he wants me to do," he explained. "And sometimes my mother gives me some errands to run, too."

"You come along when you're free," she said, and took her paper from the clip on the mailbox, and turned back toward the house. She was holding the tiny kitten in one hand now, and the cats who had been mewing and rubbing against her legs turned to follow or run ahead of her down the path. It was still a pretty odd sight, but now it only made Bart smile. A minute later, though, pedaling down the road, he quit smiling. She wasn't crazy, and she wasn't funny, either. She was just nice. Probably the only thing about her that was different from most people was that she was nicer. *Heck!* he said, imagining himself explaining her to Alec, for instance. *You think everyone has to be just like you or there's something wrong with them? She isn't even crazy about cats. She just feels sorry for them. She's just too darned kind to let 'em starve.* He could practically hear Alec saying, "How many cats did you say she's got? My gosh, what a screwball!" At that Bart paused in his imaginary conversation. Who was he talking to, anyway, Alec or himself? He'd thought she was crazy himself, hadn't he? He'd even considered rushing off before he had to encounter her. "O.K.," he said loudly and severely, and reached up one fist to knock his own head.

He was so involved in his thoughts that he almost shot past the house of his next customer. This was one of the big places, with a lawn that looked like a golf course. The house was close enough to the road that he could fold the paper and toss it. He was sure to land it on the back steps, if not on the porch. But he decided to go around to the front and make a really good impression. Anyway, he was curious. He wanted to know what kind of dock a place like this might have, and how many

27

boats they probably kept. When he'd got around to the front he saw that they had a great pier, all right. It was as big as a couple of floats put together, and there were some chairs on it and a small table under a beach umbrella. But there wasn't a single boat in sight. Maybe they hadn't got them out yet. Miss Matson was probably right and it was still too early in the season. Going back to his bike he stepped off the path and tested the lawn to see if it was as plushy as it looked. It was. It made him wish he were barefooted.

He was sure the next house was where the Doberman lived, and he fished out a couple of cookies from the pockets of his pants to have them really handy. "Carter," he said to himself and presently he saw the sign beside the hedge. The hedge was just high enough so he couldn't see down to the river. But this was one place he didn't plan to examine, anyway.

Just at first he thought the dog must be inside the house, and he was disappointed. The sooner he made peace with him, the better. Until he did, he'd have to worry about it every day. He'd started down the flagstone path beyond a gap in the hedge when the dog came out from behind a spreading bush. Bart stood still, too. "Want a treat?" Bart asked him, and held out a cookie. The dog wrinkled his nose and seemed to sniff the air between them. Then, in a motion so sudden that Bart just managed not to step back, the dog came straight up to him and snatched the cookie.

Bart held out a second one. This time the dog took it

28

delicately, almost gently, from Bart's fingers. "Good boy!" Bart said. "Good fella!" The dog sat down, clearly waiting for more. When Bart had fed him all the cookies he'd brought and the dog had taken them with perfect manners, Bart was encouraged to put out his hand. He held out the back of his hand with the fingers closed into his palm, and he did it quietly. His father had taught him never to approach a strange dog with a sudden, quick motion, and never with his hand open. That way the dog might think he was going to be hit. The Doberman came close, and sniffed the knuckles of his hand. "We're friends now, O.K.?" Bart said, although he still felt a little cautious about proceeding to the house. To his surprise, he didn't have to. The dog stretched up and took the newspaper Bart was holding under his arm and at once he turned away and began to trot with it toward the house. He was really trained! He knew exactly what he was doing. What a great dog! And what a gait he had, too. He moved with the grace of a racehorse who had sixty times as much speed as he was using.

Riding on to the next house Bart was feeling really lighthearted. He realized that from now on he'd have to bring something for the dog every day. The dog would be sure to expect it. But anyway, Bart wanted to. Not for any old bribe, but for an honest treat. Not because he was afraid of him anymore, but just because he liked him. He began to imagine how it would be to have a dog like that of his own. He imagined them going

29

around on his route together — well, going everywhere together. They'd be inseparable. Gosh, he wouldn't ever need to be afraid of anything with a champion like that beside him. No one would ever try to jump him. He imagined a gang, even — a real gang — standing aside when they saw his dog, giving him a wide berth. He could go anywhere!

He thought again about that kid who'd jumped him. He'd really handled that, all right. He'd totally won, and all on his own, too. Maybe he'd tell Alec about it after all. He thought about Miss Matson some more. He wasn't sure he could ever call her Matty, but maybe it would be all right with her if he called her Miss Matty. He thought about Saturday when he'd start learning all about the harbor and getting the hang of all that nautical lingo, and after that when he'd start building his raft in Miss Matty's yard. She was bound to let him. He was sure of it. He bet she'd be really interested. She'd probably be enthusiastic, feeling the way she did about boats, and parents, and all.

By the time he'd completed his route and started home he was feeling so great he could hardly contain himself. It certainly was about the most remarkable day he could ever remember happening — everything about it! Putting down that kid the way he had, and then meeting Miss Matty, and then making friends with that Doberman. It gave him practically a magic feeling, as if he could do anything he liked, and he was going to get everything he wanted. For the longest stretch he'd ever

30

tried he rode with no hands.

When he wheeled into the yard Alec was sitting on the back steps counting money. He was counting through quite a pile of dollar bills, and the small metal box beside him seemed to be half full of quarters and dimes and nickels. Bart's high spirits began to droop. "Where'd you get all that money?" he asked. He was feeling distinctly envious.

Alec didn't bother to answer. He didn't even look up. When he'd finished counting the bills he started in on the silver. "What are you saving for, anyway?" Bart asked next. Alec just went on putting the quarters in separate piles. "Why don't you save pennies?" Bart suggested then. "You might get an Indian head. Some of them are worth a hundred dollars apiece!"

He'd finally managed to distract his brother. "Why don't you shut up?" Alec said, glaring at him. "Now you've made me lose count."

"Why don't you take it all to the bank?" Bart thought to retort. "They'll count it for you. Then they'd prob-'ly give you one big bill that you wouldn't have to keep counting the whole time." It was the sort of superior remark that Alec himself might have made, and Bart felt briefly sharp.

Alec just said, "Wrong, as usual! You've got to count it yourself, and put it all in rolls or they won't have anything to do with it. *Marked* rolls."

Bart's spirits sank even lower. "What are you going to do with it, anyway?" he grumbled, returning to his

31

original envy. He certainly knew what he'd do with it, and he certainly wished it was his. He could probably buy all the materials for his raft right now. But to his surprise a remarkably pleasant expression had come over Alec's face. It was a bright, dreamy look, and though it didn't exactly include Bart, it didn't actually exclude him, either.

"I'm saving for a portable TV," Alec said, obviously thinking about it so hard and so happily that he couldn't resist mentioning it, even if it was a species of confidence. And the last thing in the world he ever did, normally, was to confide anything to Bart. "You don't have to plug them in! So you can take 'em anywhere — outdoors, to the beach, in a car, in a boat, in a tent — anywhere at all!"

For a minute Bart was caught up in his brother's enthusiasm, and particularly in the rare pleasure of Alec sharing it with him. It was a great moment. And then Alec had to spoil it all by saying, "You prob'ly never even heard of them!"

It was true, too. Bart hadn't. In fact he found it hard to imagine how they could work, all by themselves and without being attached to anything. But he didn't doubt Alec. And right away it occurred to him that he could even have one of them on his raft. That way he could really keep in touch with things — if he ever wanted to! "Are they very expensive?" he asked, although he really knew perfectly well what the gloomy answer would be.

Alec said, "Well, natch! What d'you think?" as if he were answering an idiot again. He certainly had gone back to normal in a hurry, and now he was looking really glum. It was hard to believe how nice everything had been only a minute ago. But Bart made one more stubborn effort to get back to where they'd practically, almost, been friends.

"Well!" he said with determined cheerfulness, "if they're so new, and all, prob'ly the price'll go down, and maybe by the time you've saved enough to —"

"Brilliant!" Alec said with sarcasm ringing in his voice. "Brilliant, my dear Watson." It was a double insult for him to haul in Sherlock Holmes. Those were just about Bart's favorite stories and Alec claimed, anyway, to have outgrown them way back. "And now," he added, "if you'll quit trying to exercise your feeble brain around me I just might get back to where I can really concentrate."

Bart pushed his bike into the garage and for a minute he considered polishing it. It didn't look so great to him at this moment and maybe, after all, that kid had been right about it. But what was the use? Nothing looked very great to him, the way he was feeling by now. And this was exactly the kind of thing his brother could always do to him. Here he'd come home feeling like a million dollars. He'd felt as if he could climb the sky! And now he felt only like crumpling up and crying, right down on the garage floor — on the hard, cold cement, stained with oil and scuffed with dirt.

33

Oh, he had to get away, all right! He forced himself to think about Miss Matty, and how he was going to build his raft after he'd learned to navigate, and then really shove off. And maybe, as he was thinking now, forever. With all these thoughts bolstering him, he was finally able to stroll out of the garage as if he were a really cool character and hardly anything could rock him. He even managed to go past Alec on the steps as though his brother didn't exist. And any day now, Bart promised himself, his brother really wouldn't exist as far as he was concerned. The thought revived his confidence, and he started in on his plan again. Finding his mother in the kitchen starting dinner he said, "Anything you'd like me to do?"

"Why that's very nice of you, Bart," she said, looking pleased.

"To tell you the truth," he decided to admit, "I'm thinking about asking for a raise. Do you think Pop might up my allowance? I mean, I do an awful lot of chores, and all, but you don't see me sitting around counting any wads of money."

"Well — " his mother considered. "Of course Alec's older, and he's got more — well, more demands on his money," she finished vaguely.

"Demands!" Bart exploded. "For Pete's sake! You mean because every time he wants a Coke he's got to buy two Cokes? And every time he wants to go to a movie he's got to pay for that Liz, too? Well that's his

34

problem, if you ask me! Why can't she pay for herself, anyway?"

"Now, dear," his mother said, sounding patient, "when you get to be Alec's age you'll feel different."

"My gosh!" Bart said. "I should live so long. If I've got to turn into someone like him, I'd rather die first. It's unfair!" he said before his mother could get in a word of protest. "That's what it is! Unfair!"

"Well, why don't you put it up to your father?" she suggested then.

"O.K.," he said, "I will. O.K." He was almost shouting. But then in a suddenly quiet tone he asked, "But do you think you could — sort of back me up?"

His mother said that she thought she could do that, all right, and Bart relaxed all over. He figured that his raise was as good as guaranteed, and he went off to his room to consider, in peace and privacy, just how much more he might ask for with any hope of actually getting it.

4

When Saturday finally rolled around it was such a cloudless perfection that Bart began to think about the Salt River as soon as he got up. He remembered what Miss Matty had said, but he found it very hard to believe there could be any of those unaccountable tides or shifty winds today, even though it still was spring. This was as serene as a summer's day, and he felt sure it was going to be almost as warm.

He briefly entertained the hope that Miss Matty might take him out for a sail after all. While he hauled on his dungarees and pulled a T-shirt over his head, he imagined himself being carried down the river under sail, and then on out into the harbor. He could practically feel the wind on his face and hear the waves slapping against the boat. "After all," he imagined himself saying to Miss Matty, "you can point out all the buoys, and markers, and everything, and I'll prob'ly learn them quicker this way." But he really knew it was a futile dream. She had only the one sailboat, and it had to be

36

scraped and caulked and painted before it could be put in the water. Otherwise it would certainly leak. For all he knew, it might even take in enough water to sink.

From the breakfast alcove at the end of the kitchen Bart could see his father out in the yard already, with about forty window screens that he'd brought up out of the cellar. He had a couple of sawhorses, too, placed rather close together on the grass beside the garage. "We don't have to *paint* the screens again, do we?" he asked his mother. He had a dismal vision of painting all morning so that by the time he might get over to work on the catboat his hand would be all blisters and his arm would be worn out. His mother said she thought that was exactly what his father had in mind. "And you know," she reminded him, "he did raise your allowance."

Bart said, "Yeah." It was a pretty decent raise, too. It wasn't quite what he'd asked for, but still it was a little more than he'd actually expected to get. So he wasn't in a very good position to complain. He contented himself with saying, "Well I hope we've got some new brushes, anyway. *Narrow* ones. And not all hard as a brick." It made him feel as if he had some rights, anyway, even if he didn't.

Outside it was just as warm as he'd expected it would be. His father was stirring a stick around in a gallon can of paint that was left over from last year, and he looked sweaty. Bart remarked that it felt like a good day for a swim. His father said he thought that was pushing the season a little. "Then how come you got the screens

37

out?" Bart wanted to know. "Just looking ahead," his father told him. "It may be raining next Saturday. It might rain every weekend for a month, and then we'd really be in trouble. Had a fly in the kitchen this morning." That was the kind of worrying that didn't appeal to Bart in the least. In fact he could hardly stand to think of a whole row of rainy weekends. It made him feel like bolting and going straight over to the Salt River now. He sat down on the next to bottom step.

"What I think," he said, "is we ought to work when it's raining and there's nothing better to do. We could paint the screens down cellar, or in the garage."

"They'll dry a lot faster out here," his father said. He stopped stirring and went into the garage. Coming out again he said, "Got us some new brushes. Shouldn't take us more than an hour, working together with these."

The brushes were narrow, and angled to get into the corners of screens or window frames. Bart was impressed, and at the same time he felt slightly cheated because now he was left without any reasonable objection. But he got up off the step. Then he had to say, "Where's Alec, anyway? I suppose he's gone to the bank to deposit all that money or something."

His father just handed him a brush and said, "Try this."

It was really neat, and nice to hold. Bart picked the top screen off the pile and laid it across the sawhorses. He was feeling a little bit interested, after all, in what he could do with a brush like this one. Just the same,
38

part of his mind was still occupied with Alec. "Why don't you get married," he imagined himself saying, "since you're so rich and all? Why don't you get married and move out? You can't seem to get along with anybody else in the world except that Liz, anyway."

This was a new idea, and for a bit his mind was fascinated by the picture of all the peace and happiness that would prevail without his brother around anymore. And that way, Bart wouldn't need to shove off. He'd have things all to himself and just the way he wanted them. Probably his mother would cook all the things he liked best, once she could quit spending most of her time fiddling with all those fancy dishes that Alec all of a sudden decided were the only things a sophisticated person could even digest. Bart pictured himself talking without anyone interrupting him and probably both his parents listening to whatever he wanted to say. No one would be borrowing his gear the whole time and then telling him it was no good anyway. He'd get a lot of things out from under his bed so he could at least see them when he wanted to, like an autographed baseball he'd had for about three years, and a pair of cowboy boots that didn't fit him anymore but were just as good as new, and some parts of an old motor that he still thought he could put together and maybe hitch onto his bike — various things that Alec couldn't look at without getting sarcastic and insulting.

It was one of his best dreams. But he wasn't able to go along with it indefinitely. Pretty soon he started reasoning. And what he reasoned was that even Alec wasn't insane enough to do a thing like getting married — even if he was old enough to have a driver's license. Besides, he was too selfish. It was one thing to pay for movies and Cokes and things he wanted himself. But Bart could just see him paying for all the food Liz ate and all the clothes she wore, and every old thing she might happen to want. *That'll be the day!* Bart told himself with conviction.

He began to think again about the river, and the raft he was going to build. It was the only thing he really cared about. So even if his brother did move out, and he wouldn't need to move out himself, he knew that he would still want to build that raft and navigate the Salt River.

He was so busy with all these reflections that he was amazed to turn back to the pile of screens and discover that he'd painted the last one, except for the one his father was just finishing. "Gosh, Pop," he said, "this really is a great brush. And now I'm going to clean it right." He surely didn't want this one to get all hard.

"Glad you appreciate it," his father said. "And now you're a free man — unless your mother's got some errands she wants you to do."

Bart crossed his fingers on the hope that she didn't, and then he tackled the brush. When he'd got it as clean as he could, he wrapped it in a cloth soaked in turpentine, put it back on the workbench in the garage, and went into the house. His mother had to turn off the vacuum cleaner before she could hear him, but then she said, "Oh, Alec's doing all the errands. He wanted to go in to the Center anyway." Bart decided to ignore the fact that Alec, as usual, was doing just what he wanted to do. Right now he was feeling too good to care, and he was about to do exactly what he wanted to do himself.

"If I make my own sandwiches," he asked now, "do you think I could take my lunch to the beach?"

His mother said she didn't see why not. "But you aren't planning to swim, are you?" she added. "Because you know the water is still going to be awfully cold."

Bart was able to truthfully tell her that swimming wasn't what he had in mind. And when she offered to make his sandwiches for him, he could also honestly say that he liked to make them. The point was that his mother thought peanut butter was enough by itself. He liked to put regular butter under it, and then jelly on top.

By the time he'd packed his bike basket and set forth it was still a long way from noon. He was pretty sure he'd told Miss Matty that he'd be bound to be busy all morning. So maybe he ought to go on to the beach, after all, and not show up at the river until she was likely to be expecting him. It would be a terrible waste of time, and all he wanted to do was to ride straight over to her place and get started. But he reminded himself that she'd probably be eating her lunch, too, and feeding the cats, and it wouldn't be right at all to barge in on her.

A couple of minutes later he discovered that he was headed for the Salt River. It seemed as if his bike was

41

just taking him that way, all by itself. *Heck,* he thought. *Why not?* He bet Miss Matty would be glad to see him, so early and everything. He might get in an hour's work before it was even time for lunch. Then he felt sure she'd let him eat his sandwiches on her pier. Just sitting by the river, and maybe dangling his feet in the water, would be great.

He put on a spurt of speed and started to sing. He really liked to sing, or whistle, sometimes — if Alec wasn't around to say, "You're a musical genius, you know it? You can make everything sound just alike! And it would take a genius to figure out what you think you're singing. What d'you get out of it, anyway?" But his own voice sounded all right to Bart, especially outdoors where he could put some power into it. Maybe he didn't have the greatest ear in the world, but there was nothing wrong with his lungs.

As he approached the Matson place he could see that a kid was standing near the mailbox. He thought it was the kid who had jumped him the other day. And he was sure of it when the kid saw him and right away started walking on up the road in the opposite direction. What was he hanging around for, anyway? Maybe he was a thief, along with everything else. Maybe he went around prying into people's boxes to see what he could find. Sometimes people put out a tip for the paper boy. Anyway that's what some of the other kids had told him. Bart began to feel as mad as though the kid had already taken something that was intended for him, instead of
42

its just being a thing he had imagined. But if it did happen, then how could he ever know? He wouldn't be able to even thank his customer, and that would make him look like a pretty crude type. The injustice of it filled him with indignation. Probably that kid never had a job in his life. Probably he just went around picking on other people and then trying to sneak what belonged to them.

At that point Bart got his first real look at the river, sparkling in the sunlight and looking even bluer than the sky. And there was Miss Matty, down at the pier. It made him feel better at once, and he even told himself that he didn't care about any old tips. He certainly didn't want anything from Miss Matty except for her to be his friend and to let him build his raft on her place.

He called out, and when she turned around he waved at her. When she waved back he started down the slope at a run. "I got off easy," he told her happily. She had a pail beside her on the pier and a fish line with no pole hanging from one hand.

"Glad to see you," she said, and she looked as if she meant it. "Now if you'll hold this line for a bit, I'll go fetch the scrapers and some sandpaper," she said, and got up surprisingly quickly. "Hope you catch something," she told him as she moved off, and he observed that the pail was empty, except for a little water at the bottom.

She hadn't been gone more than a few minutes before he thought he felt something tug at the end of the line. He realized that it might only have caught in some grass.

43

There was plenty of that, and in fact he couldn't see the line below the water. He twitched it slightly, and then started to pull it in. There was certainly something attached to it that weighed a lot more than a fishhook, whatever it might prove to be. A minute later he saw it. It was a fish. At least he supposed it must be a fish although he'd never seen such an ugly one. Anyway it didn't seem to be very lively, and he was able to haul it up onto the pier with no struggle at all. Close to, it looked even more awful, like some kind of a monster. He backed off a bit, even though it hardly moved. He couldn't think of anything he'd hate worse to do than take this thing off the hook. Just the idea of touching it made him shudder. Maybe it would be all right if he just dumped it into the pail, line and all? Holding the line at arm's length, he managed to raise the fish and then ease it over the edge of the pail.

When Miss Matty got back he was still standing there telling himself that maybe if he had a glove — a good, tough, leather one — he might grab hold of the fish. "What'd you catch?" she asked him. Bart said he didn't know. She looked into the pail. "Mmm — " she said "a freshwater fish. They get into the river now and again."

"What is it?" Bart wanted to know.

"Horned pout," she said.

"Can you eat them?"

"Oh, yes," she told him. "Some people are very partial to them. They're a kind of catfish."

45

Bart had to laugh. "Everything around here seems to be cats," he explained. "Catboat, catfish — "

She laughed with him. "I'll tell you, though," she said then, "one thing you're not likely to see on this river is a catamaran. You know what they are? Kind of a two-hulled boat. Looks like a couple of pontoons lashed together. Seems to be quite a fashion for 'em nowadays, and some people call them 'cats,' too. No relation at all to a regular catboat. More like a raft construction. And I guess that's how they originated, with a couple of logs lashed together for a float, or raft."

About all Bart heard was the word "raft." But the way she was saying it made it sound like something pretty inferior, say, to a catboat and he started worrying. In fact he was too worried to keep still. "Don't you like rafts?" he had to ask her. It would be too awful if she didn't. Maybe she wouldn't even allow one on the river.

But right away she said, "Pshaw! I was talking about catamarans. A real, honest raft is a good thing. Simple, practical — and sort of romantic, too. People have had a lot of adventures on rafts."

Bart let out a long breath of relief. Maybe now was the time to start telling her about his plan?

5

────────────

WHILE SHE WAS TALKING, Miss Matty picked up the fish in one hand and the line in the other and neatly extricated the hook from the wide, ugly mouth.

"Looks more dead than alive," she remarked. "People mostly seem to fish for horned pout after dark, with a lantern over the side. So they may be night creatures, and not very lively during the day. Then I expect this fellow got swept downriver on an outgoing tide. Maybe salt water doesn't really agree with him." She picked up the pail and dropped the fish back into it. "Well, I'll see what the cats think of him," she said and turned back toward the house. "You want to start in on the boat," she said, "take that scraper with the long handle. It'll work better — and I'm used to the old one."

The long-handled scraper looked so new that Bart wondered if she hadn't just bought it, and maybe for him. The blade looked really slick, and unblunted. Miss Matty paused to call back, "Just be sure to use it flat. You get it on the edge and it'll dig right into the wood.

We don't want to remove anything more than the old paint."

When he'd got over beside the beached boat he could see that she had already made a start on stripping it. In places it was down to bare wood, and the marsh grass was sprinkled with scraps of dried white paint. Bart really liked a black boat. He thought they always looked especially sleek, and gave an interesting piratical impression. But now that he came to think about it, he wasn't sure he'd ever seen a catboat painted anything but white. Maybe it was a kind of tradition. At least white was his second choice, for a hull. He decided to start at the bow, and when Miss Matty got back to pick up where she'd left off on the stern, they'd be working toward meeting in the middle.

There didn't seem to be any wind at all, and the sun felt hot on his face and along his arms. He tried out the scraper's edge just to be sure he knew what Miss Matty was talking about. Even used very lightly it made a noticeable scratch in the wood. He could see that with any pressure at all it would gouge like a chisel and leave real grooves. He held it flat to the boat's surface and drew it along, but still with a light pressure. When he'd really got the knack he might be able to bear down a little. Meantime he was determined to give it his full attention and not let his thoughts wander. But a few minutes later he'd started planning his conversation with Miss Matty.

Maybe the most important thing was to tell her that his

48

raft had to be a secret. He certainly had to impress that on her. So perhaps he should start be swearing her to secrecy before he even let on what he had in mind. That way he'd learn right off whether or not he could trust her. Still, he thought next, that might give her the wrong impression. She might think he was a sneaky type, or had something sinister in mind. Perhaps he ought to start by telling her about his family, and all. *I've got this brother* — he began thinking. But just then Miss Matty joined him.

"Looks as if you're getting the hang of it," she said. "Don't worry too much about the pressure as long as you keep the blade flat."

For a second he was startled, and even felt a little guilty, as if he really was a sneaky type, plotting away and hardly paying any attention at all to what he was supposed to be doing. But then he realized that he actually had made some progress on the old paint, and anyway she seemed to think he was doing all right. All in all he felt cheerful enough to say, "I guess I learn pretty fast."

Miss Matty laughed. "That's the spirit," she said. "I expect you'll make a good sailor yet. It takes some nerve, you know. Takes some confidence. The water's no place to start doubting yourself." She laughed again as if she were really pleased.

When she'd got to work with her old scraper they were silent for a few minutes, and it occurred to Bart that she was trying just as hard as he was to make the paint really

49

50

peel off and fly. He guessed that he wasn't only competing with her, but she was competing with him, too. He wanted to finish his half and get to the middle ahead of her. And by the way she was going, he guessed she had the same goal in mind. Without pausing in his work he asked, "Do we have to sandpaper after we've finished scraping?"

"That's right," she told him, and she didn't pause, either. "You getting discouraged?" she asked then.

"Oh, no," he said quickly. But it would have been more truthful if he'd said yes.

"It's a lot of work," she said, "and that's a fact. Got to do it every year, too. Now these modern Fiberglas boats — no unkeep at all! Year after year you just put 'em in the water, and that's it. And I'll tell you," she went on although she was still working fast and Bart thought she was beginning to sound just a little out of breath, "I've had some weak moments when they kind of tempted me. No work at all, and just pure pleasure! But the fact is, I hate 'em! To me they look like bathtubs, or some such equipment. No quality to 'em, in my opinion. No style! A *boat*," she said, and now he realized that the sounds of her scraping had stopped. He glanced up and saw that she had not only paused, but had come to a full stop. And her head was up, like someone watching a flag being raised, or something like that. So he knew how she felt about boats, all right. "A real boat," she said, "is made of wood. Maybe I'm old-fashioned, but that's the way I look at it."

A minute later her scraper was going again. Bart decided that he might risk an opening question. "What sort of wood," he asked, "are boats generally made of? I mean," he added, trying to conceal the direction of his actual inquiry, "this seems to be a rather soft wood. And I just wondered — "

"Cedar," she told him. "At least more often than not they're made of cedar. This one certainly is."

He made himself wait a bit before asking, "Did you ever hear of balsa wood?"

"Oh, yes," she said. "It's a particularly light wood. I don't mean light in color, but light in weight. They sell it for making model planes. That a hobby of yours?"

"Not especially," he said. "I mean, not anymore."

"Of course," she said, pursuing her own thoughts, "you don't need much for those little models. Small pieces. Leftovers, I expect. In any size, or quantity, balsa is expensive. Comes from South America, as I recall. Tropical, anyway. It's used for life preservers, and life rafts. Well, I guess it's pretty generally used for rafts."

"How expensive do you think it is?" Bart asked next.

"Goodness," she said, "I couldn't begin to guess. Never had any reason to find out."

"Didn't you ever know anyone who built a — well, a raft or anything?"

"Can't say that I ever did," she told him. "I've read about them, though. Seems to me Tom Sawyer — or was it Huck Finn — went down the Mississippi on a raft. You ever read — ?"

Bart had stopped exactly listening, and now he said, "It might be interesting — to try building something like that. I mean, if you knew where to get the materials, and all." For a minute he was afraid that she'd stopped listening, too. But then she said, a little absently, "They might know at the boatyard, I suppose. Hard to say. Doubt if there's much call for balsa — "

"Maybe you could — " Bart started to say, and then he changed it to "Maybe a person could use something else. You know, if he didn't have much money and needed a — well, a life preserver or something."

They were close to meeting now, and he was surprised to have her stop and then turn and really look at him. "I thought you told me you were a good swimmer," she said, as if she'd not only followed the entire conversation but had caught on to the fact that he was actually talking about himself and his own interest. "What do you want with a life preserver?"

"I don't!" he said. "I mean I *am* a good swimmer. I won a medal last summer — "

"I remember," she said. Apparently she listened to everything, and remembered everything, and he wasn't at all sure she wasn't a mind reader, into the bargain. He began to feel so foolish that he had to so something.

"To tell you the truth," he said, taking a firm grip on himself, "I've been sort of thinking about building a raft. Only it's got to be a secret!" he added quickly. "I don't want anybody else to know about it! Not anybody!"

"Well, that's all right," she said so calmly that he felt as if he'd been shouting, or talking like a jittering idiot. "But a raft's a pretty big thing to conceal, isn't it? You can't exactly shove it into your closet or keep it under the bed." Bart had an uneasy picture of all the things he kept under his bed. Maybe she really was a mind reader?

"What I thought," he said, in the honesty of desperation, " — maybe you'd let me keep it here?"

"Yes?" she said. He wasn't sure whether her tone was encouraging, or maybe challenging. Maybe even a little suspicious. "Go on!" she said next.

He wracked his brains as best he could on the spur of the moment. "The thing is," he said, "I didn't just pick on you, to help me out or anything! I really didn't! But I really love this river! I always have, as long as I can remember. I just love it," he said intensely. "And then, all of a sudden, I was given this paper route, right along the Salt River. It just seemed as if I was *meant* to be on the Salt River."

"I can see what you mean," she allowed. "And anyway, here you are. And I told you I'd teach you to sail. Matter of fact you can fool around with the catboat — once you learn to handle it."

"Gosh, Miss Matty," he said, "that certainly is nice of you! But I figure I ought to have something of my own. And I figure a raft is something I could build — "

"I like your independence," she said. "You plan on a sail?"
54

"Oh, yes," he told her. "Otherwise I guess I'd have to pole it, or work on the oar the whole time."

She chuckled. "Might as well let the wind do most of the work. You've really put your mind to this, haven't you?"

"Oh, I've been thinking about it for a long time," he said. He was beginning to feel confident, and even cheerful. "So I thought, if we were friends — or anyway if you didn't hate me or anything — you might let me keep it here."

She said, "Mmmm. I suppose you'd want to build it here, too?"

Bart hesitated. "Would that — bother you?" he finally asked. "Or scare the cats, or anything?"

"There's a kid around here who tries to scare cats," she told him. "Throws things at them! If I could — "

Bart was briefly distracted. "I bet I know who he is," he said. "He tried to scare me, too. I caught him fiddling with my bike — "

"I wish I could catch him," she said. "I'd give him a piece of my mind."

"I'll catch him for you!" Bart said. It made him feel good just to think about it. If he could do something sort of heroic like that — save her cats, and all — he guessed she'd be his friend forever. "He's scared of me," he told her.

For a minute she looked a little surprised. But then she said, "I guess he's scared of a lot of things — deep down, I mean. Got to be, to go around acting the way he does."

"So do you think it's O.K. and I can build my raft here?" Bart couldn't resist saying.

She seemed to be considering it, but she had a little smile around her mouth. "Don't see why not," she said finally. "Matter of fact, I think it would be interesting, too." Bart wanted to shout with joy. "Only thing —" she added, looking more serious now. "All this secrecy." Bart's spirits sank. Maybe he was going to have to tell her all his troubles after all, and he'd hoped he wouldn't have to. "You got a good reason?" she asked next. He nodded vigorously. "You strike me as pretty honest," she said, "in a roundabout sort of way. I suppose your parents disapprove?"

"I guess they would, all right," he admitted, "if they knew about it."

"They let you have a bike, though," she said, as if she were really thinking about it. "And with all the traffic there is today, strikes me you'd be a lot safer on the water. But of course that's just my opinion."

Bart picked it up in a flash. "Especially on a raft!" he said. "How could you capsize a raft?"

"Doubt if you could," she agreed. "Still, I'm not your mother."

"It's my father," Bart put in. "He's the worst."

Miss Matty sighed. After a long moment she said, "Tell you what — let's build it, anyway. And let's try
56

it out, you and me. Then we can think about it some more after that."

Bart was so delighted that it was all he could do to just say, "That's great!" Once he had the raft he was more than willing to let the future take care of itself.

Miss Matty began scraping again. "If we get this finished," she said, "we might run over to the boatyard this afternoon. Might as well ask a few questions, anyway."

6

THEY'D MADE a good start on the second side of the boat
by the time they agreed to knock off for lunch. Miss
Matty went in to fix her own, and Bart got out his sandwiches and settled himself at the tip end of the pier that
hung out over the water. The tide was still going out,
and the river was too low for him to reach the water with
his feet. But he took off his shoes anyway.

On either side of Miss Matty's place the river curved
away, and there were no other houses to be seen from
here. It gave Bart a sense of commanding the whole
scene, and as if the river belonged to him alone. For a
while he just watched the water running out to sea. He
tried to imagine how deep it might be, and he wondered
when the tide might turn. When he'd finished his lunch,
he leaned back on his elbows. Now he could scan the sky
as well as the water. With the sun hot on his face, and
the moving water at his feet, and the keen, salt smell of
the air all around him, he began to dream.

He imagined the river going on forever, with himself

58

sailing down it past houses, and marsh meadows, and occasional crowding trees, constantly winding and showing something different around every bend. It wouldn't be the same at all if it went straight like a road that somebody planned and laid out to just get somewhere as fast as possible. The river took its own way, and no hurry about it, either. Even running with the tide he guessed you couldn't move too fast along all those bends and meanders. He wondered how long the river really was. He liked to think of it as practically endless.

Still, he was interested in the ocean, too. Maybe after a couple of hours or so he'd be about ready to hit the harbor, and then the open sea. Now he imagined sailing on out, way beyond sight of land, where there was nothing but water and sky. It would be like all the space and all the freedom in the world, with himself in the middle of it. It made him feel like a giant, as if all that space had got inside of him. But then, for some reason, he suddenly thought about night. When the sun set, and the darkness took over, how would it be then?

He wasn't afraid of the dark, normally. He told himself that he wasn't. But in the middle of the ocean in the middle of the night? Well, he decided that would be like all the darkness in the world, and he guessed that was more darkness than anyone was apt to like. Even if he got to be a good sailor and could steer by the stars, then what if it was rainy and there weren't any stars? He sat up straight again, and a minute later he put his shoes back on.

59

Probably he'd have to find an island. He wanted to find one, anyway. He began to feel curious about the charts that Miss Matty talked about. They'd be sure to show all the islands along with the lighthouses and buoys and everything. Still, he wasn't sure he wanted to look at those charts just yet. They might be disappointing or something. Maybe there weren't any islands, for instance. On the other hand, he might find an island that wasn't on any map! At that moment the pier creaked behind him and he realized that Miss Matty was back.

"I've been thinking," she said. "Why don't we run over to the boatyard now? They might decide to close up early — a nice Saturday afternoon. Pretty early in the season for much business, too. Let's go."

Her car was an old jeep with outsized tires for running on sand. Bart hadn't ever ridden in a jeep before and he presently discovered that it wasn't too comfortable. Jouncy. But he liked it anyway. "I'll just ask about a float," Miss Matty said as they rode along. "Same idea. I expect you could make a float out of balsa, too. Jepson'll think my old float's giving out. No one needs to know what we've got in mind."

Bart laughed. She sounded almost as interested in his plan as he was himself. And he thought maybe she rather liked the secrecy, after all, as if they were involved in a conspiracy, and it was fun.

"Now *there's* a boat!" she said as they hauled into the yard. "Look at those lines!" It was a good-sized sailboat with two masts, and set up in a cradle, looming over them,
60

it looked enormous. It looked beautiful, too, even to Bart's unpracticed eye, and even though it was painted white. He spent a minute imagining how great it would look if it were black.

"What do you think that costs?" he asked her as they got out of the jeep.

" 'Course it isn't for sale," she said. "Someone's starting to get it ready for the water. If it was new — " she hesitated. "Well I'd hate to say," she finished. Bart decided that white was pretty dazzling, at that, with all the mahogany trim along the deck, and the bright, brass fixtures.

The tall man lounging in the open doorway of the shop said, "Howdy," and Miss Matty introduced Bart to Jepson.

As they all went inside she said, "Glad to see you've still got some real boats in the yard, anyway." Bart gathered that she was delivering some sort of a friendly insult, although he didn't understand it just at once. The shop was like a huge old barn, with sheds attached to it. The main room was stocked with every sort of small nautical equipment: anchors, bells, lights, oars, and including some apparel, like slickers, sneakers and rubber boots. One long wall was all shelves carrying tins of marine paint. Through the doorway to a shed beyond, Bart could see the outlines of various boats.

Mr. Jepson said, "Yep!" in answer to Miss Matty. "And I've got some more of the same for sale."

"Hmm," she said. "Thought you'd gone overboard for the Fiberglas jobs."

"That's right," he told her. "Haven't got another thing in the place — or in the yard, as it happens."

She whirled around and took another long look at the cradled boat outside. "You're crazy," she told him. "If that ketch is — "

62

"Well it is," he broke in. "Of course the trim's wood, all right. Take a closer look. Yep!" he said again, "lot of improvement's been going on while you were looking the other way."

Miss Matty looked blank, and disappointed at the same time. But right away she pulled herself together. "So what's it doing up there for scraping and painting?" she demanded. "I thought the whole point was no up-keep."

"That's right," he said again in his slow, drawly way. But he sounded so sure of himself that Bart was afraid Miss Matty was really wrong. "Just got to clear the bottom of barnacles and algae and stuff. Nothin' to that," he said. He grinned at Bart. "Got to keep up with the times," he said, "isn't that right, young fella?"

Before Bart could come up with any answer that suited him, Miss Matty said crisply, "Maybe *you* have to, but *I* don't." It seemed to satisfy her, as though she had somehow come out on top. "Now," she said in a business-like way, "you know anything about balsa wood?"

"What you got in mind?" he asked.

"Never mind beating around the bush," she told him. "If you never heard of it, just say so."

He shook his head in a helpless sort of way. You've got wood on the brain, Matty," he said. "Cedar wood, ash wood — and now it's balsa wood. Sure I've heard of it. Just depends on what you want it for. The hobby shops are full of it — "

"If I wanted to go to a hobby shop, I wouldn't be here,"

63

she told him. "You think I want to make a toy float — for my cats maybe?"

"Float!" he said. "Why didn't you say so in the first place? Now the best substitute — "

"Seems to me you've got substitutes on the brain," she broke in. For a second Bart thought Mr. Jepson was going to laugh in spite of himself. Anyway, he guessed the exchange of insults was a kind of game between them, and they both enjoyed it.

Mr. Jepson straightened his face and said, "You use nylon rope, don't you? You might as well say that's a substitute for hemp."

He had obviously scored a point and for a minute Miss Matty was at a loss. "Lot more expensive," she grumbled then.

"Worth more," he retorted. "Now, about this balsa wood — when I was in the Navy they used it all right — for rafts. Terrible amount of work, though. First you got to cover the wood with cement, and then you got to wrap it in canvas, and then you got to paint the canvas — two or three coats. And talk about expense! That wood comes from — "

"I know where it comes from," she told him. "All I'm asking you is where I can get it around here."

"Hanged if I know." He shrugged. "Might try the lumber yard. Might ask the Navy. I guess the government can afford it — if nobody else can."

"Nonsense!" she said. "It can't be that bad." As they

talked she had begun to edge toward the boat sheds, as if her curiosity was getting the better of her.

"Let me know when you find out," he said, "and I'll sell you something suitable. That old float of yours finally gone to the bottom?" He'd been watching her move toward the boats and now he raised his voice slightly in order to follow her. "Meantime, if you're interested in a new boat — "

She turned around so fast she bumped into Bart who was right behind her. "If I ever trade the *Catnip*," she said, "it won't be for any imitation."

Bart was beginning to think that she certainly was stubborn. But this time Mr. Jepson really chuckled. "You're a traditionalist, Matty," he said. "And you aren't the only one — "

"You aren't telling me anything," she interrupted. "Know what I think? I think you'd like to get your hands on my boat."

"Wouldn't be on my hands more'n overnight, hardly," he said in unexpected agreement. "I got two or three customers right now looking for a good old catboat. Hard to pick 'em up, anymore."

"Now you're talking," she said in a satisfied voice. At the outer door she paused to call back, "I'll give you first chance at it — if I ever see anything I like better." Out in the yard again, she went up to the cradled ketch and gave it a good, hard look. Then she reached up to touch it and run her hand along the gleaming surface. All she

65

said was, "Mmmm," but Bart knew she was convinced. "Well," she said then, "guess we may as well go back to work. Lumber yard closes on Saturdays. I'll make some inquiries on Monday. Might phone the Navy yard, if it comes to that."

Bart thought again about how stubborn she was. Only now he felt as if maybe "persistent" was a better word. In any case, he certainly was grateful for the way she was pursuing his interest for him.

Jouncing down the river road, and approaching her house, they both saw the figure of a boy not far from her mailbox, and spoke of it at the same time. "There he is again!" Bart said, while Miss Matty was saying, "Looks like that same kid, hanging around again."

She speeded up a little, and now they saw the kid turn, see them, and start off up the road at a fast clip. He was out of sight around the bend by the time they'd come to her driveway. "I'll catch up with him one of these days," Bart said as they jolted to a stop in her garage. For a minute she just sat at the wheel. "Looks as if he's got nothing to do," she said thoughtfully. "Must be new around here. I know most of the kids by sight anyway."

"Maybe he doesn't live around here at all," Bart suggested.

Getting out of the car Miss Matty said, "It's a long walk from town."

"Gosh!" Bart said. "That's right, isn't it? I mean he always seems to be walking. But he said he had a bike — a Raleigh with speeds and all."

66

"What he'd like to have, I expect." Starting down the path to the house she commented that there wasn't a cat in sight. "Generally some of 'em around," she said.

"You figure he's been scaring them again?" Bart asked. When she nodded grimly he said, "What a character! Do you think he's crazy or something?"

Miss Matty said there had to be something wrong. "And maybe we can find out what it is," she added.

The idea didn't appeal to Bart in the least. "You mean we've got to get *acquainted* with him?" He sounded as horrified as he was feeling.

She turned and looked at him. "What are you afraid of?" she asked him. "I thought you said he was afraid of you — and that's certainly the way he acts."

"I just don't like him!" Bart said. "I don't like him at all. And what I think is, the way he acts is guilty."

"I don't like his behavior," she said. "But there's got to be a reason for that."

Bart was feeling stubborn now. "Maybe he's just naturally mean," he said. "That's what I think."

Miss Matty shook her head. "Nothing natural about meanness," she said firmly. "Look at it this way — did you ever see a mean puppy?"

He hesitated. "Why do you say that?" he asked finally.

"Just because," she told him, "a puppy's such a good example of what's natural. A wriggly, friendly puppy — nothing in the world more trusting. That's the way things start. That's natural!" They'd got to the beached boat by now and she stooped to pick up her scraper.

67

"You'll get a mean dog sometimes," she said. "But that's only after someone's been mean to him."

Bart picked up his scraper, too. But she was still just standing there looking across the tall grass, almost as if she'd forgotten about him and thought she was alone. She had an odd look on her face. It struck him that she was looking sad and angry at the same time. Then she said, "It can take a long time — and a lot of abuse — to turn a friendly puppy into a mean old dog." It was as if she were talking to herself, and at the same time he knew she wasn't. He was beginning to feel uncomfortable, and he even wondered if she thought he was mean — not wanting to know that kid, and all. Just the same, in his heart he still believed that kid was just naturally mean. It made him feel defensive, and a little defiant, too. "Maybe people are different," he said.

At that moment she said, "Here they come!" in a bright, changed voice. Following her gaze he saw the cats coming up from the long, marsh grass where they couldn't be seen at all from a slight distance. Now Miss Matty was just looking pleased, as if nothing had happened and the cats were just coming back from a walk, or had been off hunting.

He started applying the scraper with a vengeance. *You wait and see,* he was saying to himself. *Any day now I'll catch up with that kid, and then you'll see for yourself!*

7

By THE TIME Bart got home it was late in the afternoon, but it was still too early for supper. As he swung into the driveway he saw that the car wasn't in the garage, and just at first he thought nobody was around. In the next minute he saw Alec, and Liz with him, on the grass at the far side of the garage. Alec was down on his knees tinkering with something that Bart instantly recognized as his own motor that he kept under his bed. Liz was standing over it and as Bart wheeled into the garage she was saying, "I just wouldn't have the *least* idea how to put all those parts together! Honestly, Alec, you're — " Bart lost the end of her sentence, but the admiration in her voice was just plain sickening in his opinion. He practically dropped his bike on the garage floor in his haste to get out to them.

"What are you doing with my motor?" he demanded.

For a second Alec looked startled, but right away he got that patient, polite look on his face that he always managed to assume when Liz was around. You'd think he was a saint, or a gentleman, or something, Bart was telling himself. "You remember Liz, don't you, Bart?" Alec said then.

Even without the unmistakable emphasis he put on the words, Bart would have got the point, all right. Alec was trying to make him look rude because he hadn't said hello to Liz, and, as usual, trying to make himself look great. Bart went right on staring at no one but Alec. "What are you doing with my motor?" he said again, although he was so furious that it was a wonder he could speak.

"In the first place," Alec said, with a maddening, exaggerated calmness, "it isn't a motor — yet. I'm just trying to figure out if all these pieces can be assembled — "

"Alec thinks he can make it work," Liz put in, "and my brother — "

Bart kept right on glaring at Alec. "It's mine," he said, "as you know darned well, and I'll put it together when I get good and ready."

Alec got up off his knees and dusted his clean chinos. "Now, Bart," he said, sounding as if he were Bart's father, at least, "You know perfectly well that these parts have been sitting under your bed for something like two years, and if you were capable of putting them together — "

"They can sit there for the rest of my life if I want them to!" Bart broke in. "They belong to me!"

Liz said, "Oh, dear! Alec was just being so *nice* — " She sounded as if she might start crying, which was about what Bart would expect of her. He guessed Alec thought

71

she might, too. Anyway, she was the only person he was really listening to, obviously. For a minute he thought Alec was going to lose his temper and act like himself, after all. Instead his brother just stood up a little taller and said, "The point is, Bart, Liz thinks her kid brother could use it on his wagon — "

"Well, he can't!" Bart practically shouted.

"Buddy's been sick," Liz said now in what struck Bart as about the drippiest voice he'd ever heard. "He had to have his tonsils out and he's just got back from the hospital, and we thought — "

Bart made himself look at her for the first time, and if there was anything that could make him any madder it was the soupy expression on her face. So he said exactly what he was thinking. "He can die as far as I'm concerned," he told her. At that she burst into tears.

For a second Bart thought his brother was going to hit him. But Liz started blubbering about how she didn't see how anyone so horrible had ever got into the same family with Alec, and then she bolted and ran off around the side of the garage. So of course Alec followed her, but not until he'd given Bart a murderous look, and one that didn't need any words to say, *I'll take care of you later.*

Bart was so upset he was shaking. He figured he was more apt to be the one to die than anyone else. He seriously wondered if anyone had ever died of rage. He certainly felt as if something was going to explode inside him. And then he had an awful feeling that he might

72

start crying, too. It was such a revolting idea that he made himself begin gathering up the motor parts to take them back into the house. And now he'd probably have to think of a new place to hide them, too.

He was just struggling through the back door when the car drove in, so he promptly dropped a couple of heavy parts, and then stumbled over them, and dropped the rest on the kitchen floor. He was still trying to pick them up again when his father pushed in the door and said, "What's all this? You starting a machine shop?"

All Bart could say was, "I hate Alec! I just *hate* him. And I — " he tried to think of exactly the right word — "I *despise* that Liz!" His father set some bundles down on the kitchen counter, and then went back to hold the door for Bart's mother and her bundles.

"Why Bart," his mother said, "that doesn't sound like you. What — "

"You just don't know me very well," he told her, although right away it made him feel so strange and lonely that he almost wished he hadn't said it.

"But what happened?" she persisted.

"Why don't you ask Alec?" he suggested. "It won't make any difference what I say, anyway."

"You seem to be feeling pretty sorry for yourself," his father remarked. "Now why don't you clear up this mess so your mother can get around the kitchen without breaking her neck, and then we'll sit down and hear your story. Fair enough?"

Bart didn't think there was anything fair going on

around this house, or anywhere else he could think of — except maybe on some island if he could just find one. He made himself think about that as hard as he could while he picked up his motor parts all over again.

He'd just gotten the last of them into his room, although he still hadn't figured out a good hiding place for them, when he heard Alec bang the back door and start shouting around the kitchen. *Why don't you go into politics,* Bart muttered to himself, *where you can shout all you want, and tell all the lies you want, and people'll pay you for it?* Still, he decided he'd better get out there right away and at least find out what he was up against.

"Look at him!" Alec shouted when Bart appeared in the doorway to the kitchen. "Of all the horrible, self-righteous monsters! You know what he did?" he demanded of his mother. "He told Liz he hoped her brother would die. That poor little kid who just got out of the hospital — "

"I didn't either!" Bart shouted back at him. "I never said any such thing. I just said I didn't care, and that's the truth. I don't. I don't even know him. I never even saw him in my life."

"Just the same, dear — " his mother began, but Bart was in no mood to be stopped, and especially with such an unsympathetic beginning.

"Everybody has his tonsils out," he said. "What's so great about that? It isn't even dangerous. I had my tonsils out but I didn't have to go around stealing other people's gear to make myself feel better."

Alec clutched his head dramatically. "Who's stealing?" he shouted. "How self-righteous can you get? That poor little kid, he can't even talk yet, hardly. He can't even swallow — so you want to deprive him of some small — "

"I'm not trying to deprive him of anything!" Bart almost screamed. "He's trying to take my motor away from me. I never heard of anything so unfair in my life! I never — "

"I never heard of anything so selfish in my life," Alec yelled back. "You aren't even using those pieces of junk, and I don't believe you ever will. You're a dog-in-the-manger, that's what you are."

"If they're all such junk," Bart retorted, "then how come you want them? Everything that belongs to me is worthless, according to you, until all of a sudden you want to borrow them, or steal them or something."

Alec appealed to his mother again. "And furthermore," he told her, "he's got the manners of a pig. A low-class pig! Do you realize that he didn't even speak to Liz? He didn't so much as acknowledge her existence! It was embarrassing. She must think I belong to a pretty crude family — "

"I don't care what she thinks," Bart broke in. "She's a hypocrite. All she does is stand around flattering you so you'll do what she wants — "

"She happens," Alec said in a suddenly cool voice, "to be a very sincere person. But you wouldn't know about that. You wouldn't understand her in a million years. And from now on it's all right with me if you never speak to her again. I advise you not to, in fact," he finished in a threatening tone, and started out of the room. But just then his father came back in from outside.

"I could have heard you in the Center," he said. "Both of you."

Bart felt overwhelmed with the injustice of it. Naturally he had to shout as loud as Alec, if he could. "I can't even defend myself around here," he said bitterly. "And nobody else is about to stand up for me," he added, giving his mother a reproachful look.

"Your mother probably couldn't get a word in edgewise," his father remarked.

"She probably wasn't even listening," Alec said, and he sounded as if he were feeling bitter, too.

"That's enough!" his father said sharply. Alec was just about as tall as his father, and bigger across the shoulders, and sometimes he looked at his father as if he'd like to remind him of those facts. He might just about as well have put it into words. His father got it, and Bart could see him getting it right now. "You go to your room and cool off," his father's voice made it an order. "And that goes for you, too, Bart," he added. Alec looked as if he was too mad to say anything, and didn't quite dare to do anything. Then he stormed out of the kitchen. A minute later Bart left, too.

If Alec ever hit his father, Bart figured that he himself would wade in and hit Alec. The way he saw it, everybody had someone to stick up for him except Bart. Alec was so crazy about that Liz he'd just as soon murder his own brother for nothing more than merely paying no attention to her. And no one could complain about his mother — even if she really hurt his feelings — without his father taking her side. And here he had no one to defend him and he couldn't even defend himself without getting everybody down on him.

His motor parts were still in the middle of his room. "They're mine!" he said again in a loud voice. Then he kicked at them, hard, as he walked around them. He'd really lost interest in them by now. They were just a symbol of all the injustice in his life. He threw himself down on his bed and stared at the ceiling and brooded. He could hear Alec's radio sounding loud enough to blast everyone out of the house.

If only he had his raft all built right now! Today was only Saturday. Tomorrow was Sunday and nothing would be open. He'd have to wait for Monday — practically two whole days — before Miss Matty could even find out about the wood he needed. Then suppose she wasn't able to locate any? Or suppose it had to come all the way from South America, or worse? He seriously wondered how long he could go on living in this family.

8

BART MANAGED to get through Sunday avoiding Alec. The feat was made fairly easy by Alec being absent the greater part of the day. No doubt, Bart told himself, he was with Liz over at her house, apologizing to her, and to her kid brother, and telling everyone what a freak his own brother was, and how he didn't even belong in the family at all. "That's all right with me!" Bart imagined himself telling Alec. "I never chose this family, and I don't plan to stick around here any longer than I can possibly help."

He wouldn't be surprised if Alec went so far as to tell everyone that Bart was adopted. It might be the truth, too. He paused to consider it. The way it looked to him, one of them had to be, and he certainly couldn't imagine anyone going and picking out Alec. He just had to be a natural misfortune that nobody had bargained for. Or if his parents had made such an awful mistake, when Alec was a baby and all, they'd surely have given him back by now. So that left Bart himself the one who had to be adopted. A very sad feeling swept over him. It

78

was as if he was totally alone in the world, related to no one, and with no one caring about him. It was such a terrible feeling that it was all he could do not to break down and cry. And the effort not to cry began to make him feel as if he was going to be sick.

He had to do something, and what he decided to do was to think. Maybe Miss Matty would adopt him? He wondered if it was possible to be adopted twice. Anyway, he thought next, if he didn't even belong to his parents they wouldn't care if he lit out. He wouldn't have to worry about them at all. He was free! He hung on to the idea of how free he was because it felt a lot better than brooding on how lonely he was. Now that he came to think about it, he guessed he'd always been alone, as far back as he could remember. So it seemed as if he ought to be used to it by now.

At that moment an unexpected picture floated into his mind. He was seeing in his imagination that kid who kept hanging around Miss Matty's place. He was always alone. Maybe he didn't belong to anyone at all? It made Bart feel so uncomfortable that he asked himself, "What's the idea?" Why did he have to suddenly remember that kid? He didn't want to think about him at all — unless he actually had to, if he ran into him again, for instance. The idea of him busting into Bart's mind, like a haunt or something, was infuriating. In fact it made him so mad that he didn't have much room left to go on feeling sorry for himself, and after a bit he realized that his spirits had begun to improve.

79

When it was finally Monday afternoon and he was ready to set out on his paper route, he was feeling great. Turning off onto the river road, he started to sing. Without exactly choosing it he found himself singing "The Star-Spangled Banner." Actually it was something he particularly liked to sing, partly because everyone else seemed to think it was so difficult. He didn't have any trouble with it! As far as he was concerned it wasn't any harder than "Yankee Doodle." It was pretty similar, in fact, except for the words — and Bart liked the words better. All that about the "ramparts we watched," and then the "war's desolation" and all, gave him a keen, shivery sort of feeling, like listening to a brass band.

Just at first it looked to him as if there was no one around at Miss Matty's, not even a few cats. It was as quiet as a deserted place, like a summer camp out of season, sort of sleeping in the afternoon sun and waiting for someone to come and wake it up again. But he told himself, a little anxiously, that it couldn't be like that. It was Miss Matty's home! She lived here all the time. And now that he came to think about it, how could she ever go away? He had a brief, crazy picture of her traveling to New York, for example, with about twenty-five cats. It was obviously nutty, so what was he worrying about? Just the same he ran down the slope toward the house, and only checked himself long enough to peer into the shed that she used as her garage. Her jeep was there. So maybe she was down by the water, working on the boat again.

Well, the boat was still there, all right, and it was looking quite a lot better. He guessed that over the weekend she must have put on a first coat of paint. But where was she? Unless she was behind that pile of lumber at the far side, between the boat and the river. And that was a funny thing! It looked as if someone had wrecked a barn, for instance, and piled up the timbers on the spot.

In something like the next minute Bart had another thought. It was more like a wild hope, and it sent him really racing down the remaining distance.

When he'd come up short beside it, he discovered that it was a pile of both logs and boards. They looked fairly new, too. As a matter of fact, they looked like the makings of a raft. A really great raft! How do you like that? he asked himself. And he liked it so well that it made him give out with a whistle.

A second later Miss Matty rose up from the other side of the pile. "Glad to see you, Bart," she said. "I figure you can help me to spread this tarp." She was holding on to the edge of what Bart recognized as a large tarpaulin. "Thought I'd get this lumber covered up for the night, anyway. Weather won't do it any harm," she went on, "but I've learned that building materials can be quite a temptation. Someone picks up a piece here, and a piece there, and next thing you know you're out of wood."

Bart had been looking it over, and now he said, "How long are these logs?" It struck him that they were almost

81

as long as telephone poles, and he didn't think they'd be easy to handle.

Her answer was indirect. "I want 'em plenty long. Don't want anyone getting up on the roof except the cats. That's the point."

Bart said, "The roof?"

"Oh, I guess I haven't had a chance to tell you," she said. "I decided to put up a boat shelter. Got thinking about it when I was over at the lumberyard. Just a simple lean-to kind of construction. But it came to me it would be a handy place for the cats to get out of reach of stray dogs, and the like. No trees around — but they'll go up these logs just as if they were trees. And nothing can follow them!"

All Bart could think of to say was, "Oh." He was feeling very disappointed, and a little hurt, too. He guessed she didn't care about him and his raft, after all. All she cared about was her cats. He tugged at the tarpaulin in a dutiful, uninterested way.

"Went over there," Miss Matty said next, "to find out about balsa." Bart's interest picked up again. "No use," she said. "Jepson was right. If we could get hold of it at all, it would cost a small fortune. Luckily, though," she went on, "we've got plenty of alternatives." Bart thought of her word "substitutes," but he managed not to say it. "The point is the flotation," she said. "Right?"

The word was new to him. "You mean it's got to be buoyant?" he said.

82

She nodded. "But the wood doesn't have to be," she told him. "Now a lot of people just use sealed-up oil drums under the planking. You've probably seen them used for diving floats."

"Yeah — " he said cautiously. Any diving raft he'd ever seen was a stationary thing, to start with. "What are the other — er — alternatives?" he asked then.

"You can use driftwood," she told him. "There," she said, and straightened up, having tucked in the tarp to her own satisfaction. "Driftwood's really light, too," she went on. "Already soaked up all the water it's going to, I expect. And that wouldn't cost you anything — but the trouble of collecting it in suitable pieces."

This suggestion appealed to Bart a lot more than those clumsy old oil drums, or barrels. "I never thought of that," he admitted. "But how would I haul it — I mean from way up on the outer beach, and all?"

"We could use the jeep," she said. "However — " she started off toward the pier and Bart went along. "There's something called Styrofoam," she said. " 'Course it's one of those manufactured materials — " she turned to give him a look, "and I wouldn't let on to Jepson that I've got any respect for it!" she told him. "But between you and me, there's a lot to be said for it. Not too expensive — nothing like balsa — and it's light as a cork. Carries an amazing amount of weight, too. I think they told me that one square foot will float a hundred pounds. How do you like that?"

"Gosh!" Bart said, "that sounds great. But what does

it look like, though?" He didn't want his raft to look like a bathtub, the way Miss Matty said about some of those new boats.

She chuckled. "You're as bad as I am, Bart," she said. "You know those coolers people take on camping trips? I guess that's what they're made of. Anyway that's what it looks like. But the thing is, it doesn't have to show!"

"How come?" he wanted to know.

"You put it underneath, where it's in the water. And use your planking on top."

They'd got out to the end of the pier, and now she reached down to twitch the fish line she'd left attached there.

"But how do you fasten it to the wood?" Bart asked. "It doesn't seem as if nails — "

"Glue!" she told him. "You use a kind of glue. Sounds easy enough, and apparently it works." She sat down and took the fish line into her hands. It looked as if she planned to stay there until she'd caught something. Bart thought a little uneasily about the rest of his paper route. But his curiosity wasn't entirely satisfied yet.

"You figure I could put driftwood on top?" he asked now.

"Could, all right," she agreed. "But I'll tell you — while I was about it I ordered some extra planks. Won't cost you as much where it's all in the same lot."

Bart was so surprised, and so grateful, that he hardly

knew what to say. He ought to have trusted her! Still, he wished she had said so in the first place, and showed him his planks and all. He'd certainly like to see them! And now he'd probably have to wait till tomorrow. He looked back to the mound of lumber under the tarp that covered it like a blanket. "Golly!" he said with feeling, "I'm sure glad we covered it up!"

There it was, the actual, real beginning of his raft that had been only a dream in his mind for so long. He'd almost like to spend the night there, watching it. But right now he had to finish delivering his papers. In fact it occurred to him that he'd better keep his mind on his job since he was already, suddenly, in debt. "What do you think — I mean how much do I owe you so far?" he asked her.

"Haven't got the bill yet," she said. "And then I'll have to figure out your share. But I don't think it's going to ruin you. The Styrofoam may run to a bit more. You want to decide on that, I'll order it for you tomorrow."

"I guess I should," he said. "Is that what you think?"

"Looks like the best solution to me," she told him. "But we won't mention it to Jepson! I'd never hear the end of it."

Bart finally tore himself away although his head was still buzzing with questions, and plans. He wondered about a sail. And then should he figure on an oar, too? And would he need an oarlock, or some way to support the oar and keep it in place? He was so preoccupied

85

that he almost shot past the house of his next customer. He skidded to a stop on a stretch of loose sand, dropped his bike and started back for the gap in the hedge.

Just as he turned into the walk, from one side of the hedge someone jumped out at him shouting, "Boo!"

9

THE MINUTE BART COLLECTED HIMSELF he felt foolish. It was such a silly, little-kid trick. He wouldn't expect anyone more than about six years old to spring out at a person and say "Boo!" But it really had startled him, just the same, and he was sure he had jumped. After all, his thoughts were somewhere else altogether. And then it was so totally unexpected. All this rushed through his mind, in his own defense, but still he felt foolish, and it made him mad.

Of course it was that same kid again. That didn't surprise him any! Right away the kid had stepped back, to get out of reach, and now he was just standing there with an idiotic grin on his face. Maybe he really was an idiot? Or maybe he was actually about six or seven years old and just all overgrown like some kind of freak. But Bart really knew better. "What's the matter with you?" he said.

The kid went on grinning. "I'm fine," he said. "What's the matter with you? You sure scare easy."

"I don't scare at all," Bart told him. "I guess you can startle anyone — if that's your idea of something bright."

"Oh, for Pete's sake," the kid said, "can't you take a joke?"

"I don't know," Bart said. "Why don't you tell me one?" It made him feel cool. And the kid wasn't grinning any longer.

"Wise guy!" the kid said a little feebly.

"I just use my brains," Bart told him. "If you've got any, they certainly don't show." He gave the folded newspaper a neat toss and landed it on the back porch steps. Now he could walk away without actually turning his back and risking another tackle. But he hadn't even mentioned the subject that was really on his mind. And he'd promised Miss Matty that he would do something about it, too. He thought about her, hard, so he could really sound off with some authority. "I'm warning you," he said then. "You keep away from Miss Matson's place! If you ever throw another stone at any of her cats — well I'll take care of you!"

"You and who else?" the kid said, but he was shuffling his feet and not really looking at Bart, and it came out sounding like a pretty weak challenge.

"Me and judo!" Bart told him. "Remember?" He started to move toward his bike while still keeping an eye on the kid, so he caught the new look that had come into his face.

"Hey!" he said, and his voice had picked up, too.

"I'll make a deal with you. You teach me judo and I'll leave the cats alone. O.K.?"

Bart felt disgusted. Deals! Bargains! Bribes! "You'll leave the cats alone *period!*" he snapped back. He'd eased himself through the gap in the hedge, and now he was able to pick up his bike. But the kid's voice had followed him, and now he saw that he was outside the hedge, too. About all Bart heard was the word "mean."

"Mean?" he echoed. *"You're* the mean one! Why don't you at least pick on something your own size? How would you like it if some monster about forty times as big as you are started heaving rocks at you? I just wish some dinosaur or something would take out after you. I just wish — "

The kid started laughing like a madman. "They're extinct!" he said then in a very superior way. "Haven't you heard? Dinosaurs — and all those monsters — they're extinct."

"I wish you were extinct!" Bart told him furiously. The kid stopped laughing. "And if you go on acting like a monster," Bart went on, "that's probably just what'll happen to you, too!" It satisfied him pretty well as a parting shot, and he was about to shove off when he was arrested by the look that had come into the kid's face now. It was an awful look, a crumpled sort of look. It was almost as if he was going to start bawling. Bart was too astonished to say anything. In a way he wanted more than ever to just leave, right now. But he couldn't

89

seem to make himself move. He was too embarrassed, or something like that. He started twanging his front-wheel spokes with the toe of one shoe, and looking away and then looking back again. What he hoped was that he'd been mistaken and the only thing this kid was looking was mean, as usual. He wasn't looking mean, though. What he looked was more as if he hurt some place. In fact he looked as if he hurt all over. So the next thing Bart knew he started to feel mean himself. He resented it, and he did his best to resist it. Who started the whole thing, anyway? And what did it really have to do with Bart in the second place? Bolstered by all those thoughts he finally hit on a way out of his own dilemma. "You feeling sick or something?" he asked. He figured that was reasonably sympathetic, but it certainly put the responsibility right where it belonged, on the kid himself.

The kid didn't answer his question, but anyway he found something to say at last. And what he said was, "I'm big for my age. But I'm not a freak or anything! I'm not any monster, like you said —" his voice faltered. "Anyway not yet," he managed to finish.

"I wasn't talking about your *size*," Bart told him. Then he had to add, stubbornly, "You're an awful lot bigger than a cat, though, which is all I was reminding you."

"I never hit one," the kid said.

Bart shrugged. "Maybe you're a rotten shot."

The kid sort of winced. "That's what you'd have to

think, all right," he said. "You really hate me, don't you?"

"My gosh!" Bart said. He was feeling exasperated again. "Did I jump you when your back was turned, and the very first time I ever saw you? Did I insult your bike — "

"I haven't got a bike," the kid broke in.

"Well if you did have, I wouldn't insult it," Bart told him in a calmer tone. He was remembering what Miss Matty had said, and he was feeling uneasy enough anyway, all on his own. Whatever he was apt to say at this point wasn't likely to suit him. "I've got to finish my paper route," he announced, and straddled his bike.

"If I hated you," the kid said, talking fast so he could finish before Bart took off, "I'd know why."

Bart hesitated. He was curious in spite of himself. "O.K.," he said then, "why?"

"Because you think you're so great. I guess you like yourself so well that nobody else needs to like you."

Bart was speechless. He felt as if the wind had been knocked out of him and he couldn't speak even if he had anything to say. He'd never picked a fight in his life! He'd never picked on anyone. All he wanted was peace. All he'd ever wanted was peace and privacy. Alec came into his mind. But right away he told himself that Alec didn't count! He was crazy. Still, he was remembering Alec calling him "self-righteous." Was that what this kid meant, too?

The kid had turned and started off down the road,

but not going fast this time. He wasn't going fast at all. And now it came to Bart that there was something he wanted to say, after all. There was something he absolutely had to get straight. "Hey, kid!" he called after him.

The kid stopped and turned around, at least partway. "My name's Bill," he called back, not so much like a correction but more like just a fact. Still, it wasn't exactly like that, either. He stayed right where he was standing, and Bart stayed right where he was straddling his bike and they stared at each other. It struck Bart that the kid looked different. He wasn't looking tough, and he wasn't looking mean, and he wasn't grinning. He didn't seem to have any expression at all on his face, and this way he looked a lot better.

Bart scuffed at the sand with one foot, and then with the other. He was trying to remember what it was he had wanted to say only a minute ago. He knew it was something important, but right now he couldn't think what it was. He bounced a couple of times on the padded leather seat of his bike. Then he rose up and brought his weight down on one pedal. "My name's Bart!" he called back, and pushed off in a scatter of loose sand that rattled against his mudguards.

Riding along Bart told himself that here he was *acquainted*, probably, the way he'd told Miss Matty he certainly didn't want to be. He figured if he hurried he could swing back by her place before going home. He'd like to tell her — he'd like to ask her — well he had a lot on his mind. He thought about himself, and then he thought about that kid — Bill — and then he tried to think about himself some more. It seemed as if he had a whole pack of feelings jolting around inside him and not one of them made any sense. Maybe Miss Matty — maybe if he told her all about what he said, and what Bill said, and — anyway if he really hurried he might get a look at his new lumber! He reminded himself that it was all he really cared about.

10

IT WAS LATER than he'd thought it would be by the time
Bart had delivered his last paper. He decided he'd better
go straight home and not try to detour by Miss Matty's.
He was beginning to feel hungry, for one thing. Then,
she might have got his Styrofoam by tomorrow and in that
case he could see all his materials at the same time. He
changed his mind, took the short route for home, and began to imagine what his mother might be fixing for supper.

On the way to pick up his papers the next afternoon
he was struck by a practical thought, and it was a gloomy
one. They hadn't even talked about how much styrofoam he was going to need, so how could Miss Matty
have possibly ordered it? He was disgusted with himself for not having thought of it before. In fact now that
he came to face it, he realized that he hadn't ever once
exactly planned on how big his raft ought to be.

Miss Matty was up by her mailbox on the road when
he got to her place, and he'd hardly greeted her before
she said, "I was hoping that delivery truck might get
here ahead of you."

94

"You mean you ordered my Styrofoam?" he asked her. "But we didn't even decide how much I was going to need. I just thought about it."

"So did I," she told him, "after you'd left. But I found out yesterday — forgot to mention it — that you can get it in eight-foot lengths. Three feet wide. So I figured you'd want two, anyway. You put 'em side by side and you've got eight feet of length and six feet of width. Or, end to end you'd get sixteen feet of length and three feet of width." Bart was trying to picture it. "Seems to me," she went on, "eight by six would give you a nice, handy raft, with a little space left over. So I ordered two sections," she finished.

"Gosh, that's great," he said, "but if I wanted it longer — I mean if it was going to be sixteen feet long and then only three feet wide, well that would be kind of skinny, wouldn't it? And it would be pretty narrow to move around on much, don't you think?"

"I guess those proportions wouldn't be too good," she agreed.

"So," he picked it up quickly, "if it's going to be sixteen feet long then it ought to be anyway six feet wide. How many sections would that take?"

"Four," she told him. "You don't seem to be visualizing it too well."

"Not too well," he admitted.

"Come down to the house," she suggested, "and we'll get out the yardstick. Or, tell you what — I'll show you

95

a rug that's eight by six. That'll really give you the size, and no guessing."

Following her down the path to the house he said, "How long is the catboat?"

After a second she said, "Hmm. If I tell you how long it is, then you'll want to know how wide it is. But you can't go by that!"

"I don't see why not," Bart protested.

"Because it isn't a raft," she said. "A boat's got a hull, in the first place. A hollowed-out hull. Then, in the case of a *sail*boat the amount of sail is related to the boat's measurements, and weight."

"But I'm going to have a sail, too," Bart reminded her.

"The point is," she said, sounding stubborn, "you can't compare them! What a sail will do for a raft —"

"You mean it won't work?" he put in anxiously.

"Oh it'll give you some help all right," she said. "But you can't expect it to work exactly the way it works with a sailboat." She stopped just outside her front door. "What I mean about the length of the catboat," she said, "well, you just can't build a raft from the measurements of a boat."

Bart said, "O.K.," although he was far from totally convinced.

He'd never been inside her house and just at first he thought he'd like to go right outdoors again. It wasn't only the cat-fur smell. That tickled his nose and made him feel like sneezing. But he could also smell liver cooking, and fish cooking, and he didn't know what
96

else, all simmering away in little pots on the top of her stove. It was hard to see how she could stand it, and he even had a weak moment of wondering, all over again, if she wasn't just a little bit crazy. But he knew that she spent most of her time out of doors. He'd known that the first time he saw her, just by looking at her.

She peered into the various pots, turned off the gas under a couple of them, and then said, "Now! I can get out my yardstick, but you'll get a much better impression from that rug. In front of the fireplace." She indicated, by a sweep of one arm, the other end of the room. "That's six by eight feet, exactly."

To Bart it seemed like a funny room, with the kitchen an extension of the living room. No division, no partition. But, apart from the smells, he liked it! It was a long room that seemed to go across the whole front of the house. And he decided that it was a pretty neat arrangement, like the living quarters on a ship, maybe. And the fireplace was certainly great! All made of huge, flat stones, it covered the whole end of the room. There was a sofa at one side, and a couple of stuffed chairs at the other, along with some shelves of books. But there wasn't anything sitting on the rug except for a couple of cats, staring into the empty fireplace as though it were bright with fire, and warm. There was a cat sleeping in each chair, and three stretched out on the sofa.

Miss Matty said, "Why don't you try it for size? Just sit down in the middle of that rug and imagine that it's a raft. You got a good imagination?"

Bart had to laugh. It seemed to him that imagining was about the best thing he did. He'd certainly had enough practice to be a real expert. He managed to sit down close to the rug's center without disturbing the cats. After a minute he tried stretching out flat. There was still plenty of room for him, even with his arms extended. He sat up again and tried to imagine a sail. Maybe the first thing, though, would be an oar. He looked over his shoulder. Miss Matty was standing back there watching him. "I guess you'd mount an oar at the stern?" he asked her.

She nodded. "You know how to scull?"

He settled for saying, "I've never tried it."

"Then you don't," she told him. "It's a real knack. You've seen fishermen coming in with a single oar at the stern of the dory? That's sculling, and they can go fast, and they can go straight — without much effort, too. It's all in your wrists. Less work than rowing, once you get the hang of it."

"How would I mount the oar, though?" he asked next.

She considered it. "Seems to me," she said then, "I'd try the principle of an old-fashioned rowlock. A couple of stout pegs set in like a V. Oar fits between 'em. You still see it sometimes on an old dory."

Bart had never seen anything but the modern, metal oarlock, U-shaped to fit the shaft of the oar. Picturing them both he said, "I should think sculling would be easier with a U-shaped oarlock. I mean — "

"I see what you mean," she broke in. "The oar would

99

revolve better in something really shaped to it. And that's a basic difference between rowing and sculling. Good for you, Bart! I don't think you're going to waste much time picking up *that* knack." He was so pleased it kind of embarrassed him. While he was turning away and standing up again she said, "I guess the thing to do would be to mount it on a block, in that case. Buy the oarlock and make the block for it. You stand up for sculling," she went on, "so you'd have to get it at just the right height."

"But couldn't I steer with the oar, too?" he said. "If the current was taking me — or the wind in my sail — I could just steer with the oar. And I should think I could sit down for that."

"Expect you could," she agreed. "Though you might want the oar at a different height then."

"So, two blocks and two oarlocks," he said. He laughed. "Perfect! 'Cause I'm sure I'll have to buy a pair of oarlocks, and this way I won't be wasting one." A second later he said, "Gosh! I better get on with my route. If people start complaining that their paper is always late, I might lose my job."

Miss Matty went outside with him, and scanned the road. "May not see that truck till tomorrow, at this rate," she said. "Seems to me," she said next, "there was something else I wanted to speak about." She started strolling along with him up the slope. When they got in sight of his bike she said, "Oh, I remember now. It was about that kid."
100

Without looking at her Bart said, "His name's Bill."

He knew he'd surprised her, but she only said, "Bill Stark. What else did you find out?"

Now Bart was the one who felt surprised. But it wasn't a subject that he wanted to get into. Miss Matty's interest, in fact, only further dampened his own. Why did she care? What was it to her? In Bart's opinion she had plenty to worry about with her cats and her boat, and helping him to build his raft. "I don't think he's very interesting," he told her. He was aware that she had turned and glanced at him.

"Why do you say that?" she asked him presently.

"Oh — " he answered vaguely. "He's sort of a freak, I guess. I don't hate him or anything. I mean I really don't, anymore," he told her. "Prob'ly he can't help being all overgrown — except for his brain."

They'd got up beside his bike at the edge of the road, and now they both stopped. Miss Matty said then, "Bart, I asked you what else you'd found out, besides his name. Now, why don't you ask me?"

He knew the true answer very well. He didn't care! He didn't want to know. He wished he'd never met up with that — that Bill — in his life, never mind having to get acquainted with him! He squirmed and struggled and came up with a feeble "O.K." although he hated himself for doing it, and he hated all politeness in general. It was just pure hypocrisy, that's what it was! It was just like that awful Liz — only he really knew better, so he guessed that made him even worse.

101

Miss Matty sighed. "I guess poor Bill was just trying to make friends all the time," she said. Bart shot her a look that might have withered her on the spot like a death ray or something. Only she wasn't looking at him. "That's just plain crazy as far as I'm concerned," he managed to tell her although all he felt like was gagging.

"But look at it this way — " she said patiently. "He certainly attracted your attention, didn't he?"

"Well — sure — " he admitted grudgingly. "But all he had to do was say 'Hi' or something like that."

Sounding even more patient she said, "Maybe he was afraid you'd snub him. You see he's new around here, just as I thought. As a matter of fact he's only visiting," she went on. "He's staying with an aunt and uncle."

Bart was curious in spite of himself. "How come?" he wanted to know. "It isn't vacation, or anything."

"Some sort of family trouble, I'm afraid," Miss Matty said. "So, you see — " she started up again, but Bart wasn't about to listen to any more sympathy stuff. If he did, he figured he'd really throw up.

"What about the cats?" he demanded. "I don't see any excuse for him throwing stones at your cats. I don't see any *connection*, to tell you the truth!"

"But feelings aren't always logical," Miss Matty said.

He started to say *Mine are!* But he stopped, because in the first place it sounded pretty superior, even to himself. And in the second place he secretly admitted that

102

it wasn't quite true. He reached for his bike and stood it up.

"If you feel bad enough," Miss Matty was going on, "you can take it out on almost anyone, or anything. It doesn't have to make sense."

Bart threw one leg across his bike. "He doesn't have to make friends, either," he said, " — and if that's the way he goes about it — jumping people, insulting their gear, scaring their cats — "

"But don't you see," she said, sounding more discouraged now, "he was probably trying to make an impression — "

"He made an impression on me all right," Bart told her. "Honestly, Miss Matty, I don't see how you can defend him!"

"I never defended his behavior," she reminded him. "I just said there had to be a reason for it."

Bart said, "Mmm." He was pretty tired of the whole subject, and now that she thought she'd got it all figured out, maybe they could both forget about it. "Anyway," he told her, "I don't think he's going to bother the cats anymore." Before she could ask him why he thought so he said, "Did you order some glue for the Styrofoam, too?"

He'd distracted her enough so that she glanced up the road again. "Yes I did," she said then. "So from now on it's up to you — including the oarlocks and an oar. Why don't you go around to the boatyard one of these afternoons and pick them out?" Was she letting him know that she had given him all the help she planned to give him, and he was on his own now? He guessed that would be fair enough. After all, it was his raft, and up to now he hadn't taken much initiative about it. But he certainly hoped she wasn't going to suddenly lose all interest. With that worry gnawing at him, he started to push off. Then Miss Matty said, "Just don't make the mistake of thinking the heavier oars are the stronger ones. It's just the opposite! Better wood in the light ones." Bart relaxed. "Well, you'll find that out," she added, "because the light ones cost more, to start with." So he decided that she was still with him all right.

Maybe tomorrow, he was thinking as he pedaled down the road, he could get over to the boatyard. Then he'd have everything, and he was pretty sure it wouldn't take him long to put it together. By the end of the week — by Saturday, maybe — he might have his raft all made. Even if he didn't get the sail right away he could probably try out the raft. The oar was all he actually needed. As long as he had something to steer with he figured he might go a little way down the river anyway. Sort of a trial run. The thing to do would be to pick an outgoing tide. Thinking a little further he decided it should be the end of the outgoing tide. That way, when the tide turned he'd be able to ride back in with it.

Just the idea of it made him feel like shouting. So he began to sing.

11

BART WAS SO OPTIMISTIC about the way everything was going that he felt sure Saturday would be the day, and he'd better plan toward getting it off. If he worked like mad all week, doing chores and errands, he figured that come Saturday he'd be free to say he wanted the day off. He didn't believe his mother would ever catch on that he had anything special in mind. The worst she might do would be to tease him a little about how he must be feeling sick, or something. How about his father, though? He wasn't so easy to fool. He was just naturally a more suspicious type. Bart could imagine him saying, "What's your scheme? You going to hit me up for another raise?" And if his pop didn't happen to notice the way he was knocking himself out and all, then his brother was bound to. He could practically hear Alec saying, "What's the snow job all about?" Then even his mother might get suspicious. So he guessed the only thing to do was to more or less level with her. He didn't plan to really *tell* her anything — just to put in his bid for Saturday. If she agreed to the bargain in advance, then it was settled, and he was really in.

Just before his father got home, and after Alec had got through arguing about borrowing the car and shoved off to his room, Bart moved into the kitchen, where his mother was apt to be alone for a few minutes, anyway. "What I want to know — " he started out, " — will you make a bargain with me? It's fair!" he added hastily. "I mean anyone would have to admit that it's fair."

"Then why don't you tell me what it is," she suggested.

"I will!" he said. "I mean, I'm going to. Only I just want to know if you're feeling pretty fair right now."

Between the stove and the refrigerator she paused and really looked at him. "Don't you think I'm usually fair?" she asked him.

"Oh, sure," he told her. "I mean *you* are, mostly. But you know Pop is — well he's sometimes pretty prejudiced."

His mother smiled slightly. "I'm not sure it isn't the other way around," she said. "Your father's very reasonable. He *thinks* about things, and — sort of weighs them."

"Yeah," Bart said, "but I don't like to be all that weighed all the time."

His mother said, "Mmm. Well, why don't you tell me what you've got on your mind, and if it's as fair as you say — "
106

"Oh, it is!" Bart assured her. "It really is." He took a deep breath and plunged in. "If I do about a million chores all week, can I have Saturday off? I mean the whole day."

"Well!" his mother said, as if she was surprised, or relieved or something like that. "It sounds reasonable enough to me. In fact I don't see what you were so worried about," she added. But Bart himself knew the real source of his anxiety, and in the next minute the subject came up. "I'm just a little curious," his mother said, "about what it is you want to do all day Saturday."

Bart quit stalking around the kitchen and dropped into the nearest chair. A second later he got up again. "Well I've got this customer — " he began. "I mean she's my friend. But she isn't a kid. I mean, she's pretty old. I guess she's about as old as you, Mom." His mother looked at him again and the expression on her face made him decide he'd better say something else. "But she isn't pretty, though, like you," he said. His mother's expression improved a little. "So my friend — Miss Matty," he went on. "She's got all these cats. She isn't really crazy or anything," he felt as if he had to explain. "She just feels bad about them starving and all. So she keeps taking them in. Know what I mean?" His mother nodded a little vaguely. "So she wants to build a shelter — " he almost said that it was actually a boat shelter, but just in time he decided against that. "I mean dogs chase them and all. So I said I'd help her,"

107

he finished, and then he sat down again. It was true!
Everything he'd said was true, he reminded himself
while he waited for his mother's reaction.

"That sounds very nice," she said slowly. He got the
impression that she was still thinking about it and hadn't
quite finished what she wanted to say. He was right,

too. "I don't know," she said next, "how much you know about building — She isn't going to pay you, is she?"

It hurt his feelings and it made him feel guilty all at the same time. "Gosh," he grumbled, "you sound just like Pop. How come you're so suspicious all of a sudden? I wouldn't want her to pay me! I'm just going to *help* her — "

His mother reached out and ruffled his hair. "That's very sweet of you," she told him. "I guess you must really like her."

Now all he felt was guilty, and very uncomfortable. But he hadn't lied! He had to tell himself all over again that he hadn't lied. All he'd said was true — as far as it went. And he just couldn't go any further. It was too important. There was too much at stake. It would be the end of his whole dream, and no one could expect him to plan and work and save up — and then just ruin it all! And why? For no reason at all except that his father had this insane prejudice against the Salt River. Miss Matty *knew* the river. She lived on it! Probably she'd lived there all her life. And she thought riding a bike was a lot more dangerous. Still, he didn't feel as jubilant as he had expected to when he finally said, "So it's O.K. and I can have Saturday off," not really making it a question.

His mother said that she didn't see why not. "And now if you'd like to start being helpful around here," she suggested, "why don't you set the table." He began to feel better, and he was more than ready to start right

109

in on his end of the bargain because he figured that would clinch it.

By Saturday Bart had forgotten that he'd ever felt a twinge of guilt. He had worked like a madman all week, raking the yard and burning trash and sweeping the garage and clearing out the cellar, until it seemed to him that he must have earned more like a week's vacation than one day off.

He'd kept praying about the weather and crossing his fingers every time he thought of it. He wished his father had never mentioned that it might rain every weekend for a month. It was a possibility that Bart didn't even want to know about. But Saturday turned out to be clear and sunny, and Bart's spirits were as unclouded as the day. All he was feeling now was pure joy. It seemed as if he could burst with it. But he managed not to start singing until he got well away from the house, and from Alec who was out in the driveway washing the car.

In fact he felt so great that it didn't really bother him to find Bill scuffling along the road near Miss Matty's place. He said "Hi" to him, and he meant to just keep right on going. But when Bill said, "Gee — Hi!" and looked so darned pleased, Bart slowed up. He didn't exactly want to slow up and he certainly didn't plan to stop. But somehow or other he stopped, just for a minute. "It sure is a great day," he said. "It makes you feel good."

"I guess it would," Bill said, "if you had anything to do."

"Yeah, I guess that's right," Bart agreed. He wished he'd kept going the way he meant to. Here he was feeling uncomfortable already, and it wasn't any of his fault. Why didn't the kid get a job, for instance?

"That's a great bike," Bill said unexpectedly. "I guess you could put gears on it if you wanted to."

"But I don't really need 'em, though," Bart told him. "I can really travel! I mean it goes even better than it looks. Would you — why don't you try it?" At once he distrusted his own impulse. Just because he was feeling so good, and kind of flattered, too, was no reason to hand over his bike. "I mean just up the road," he said, "and if you'll no kidding bring it back."

"What do you think I am, a thief or something?" Bill said, sounding a little hurt but looking pretty eager at the same time.

"I don't know you very well," Bart reminded him. "But I guess Miss Matty does. I mean I guess she knows where you live, and all." That ought to do it, he told himself.

Bill began to dig into the watch pocket of his dungarees, and what he came up with really surprised Bart. "You can time me," Bill said, handing over a big, flat watch in a shiny gold case. "And if I don't come back — well I guess my watch cost at least as much as a bike. It's got an alarm, even. It rings if you set it."

111

Bart said, "Gosh! I never heard of an alarm-clock watch. Where'd you get it, anyway?"

"From my grandfather," Bill said. "It's German. How long you going to be here?"

Bart was definitely impressed with the watch. Actually, he envied it. He wished it were his. Still, it wasn't a bike! And even if it cost just as much — which he didn't doubt — he bet Bill would rather have a bike, too. So he said cautiously, "I don't know. Maybe half an hour."

"O.K.," Bill said. "You can time me," he repeated, and reached for Bart's bike.

Bart pocketed the watch, let go of his bike and said, "O.K. I'll be down by Miss Matty's pier, and we'll swap back." He stood for a minute and watched Bill wobble a bit, catch his balance and then speed off up the road. He seemed to be pedaling as hard sitting on the seat as Bart could only do by standing up. He was strong, all right. He'd be very hard to beat in a race. Bart guessed he'd be impossible to beat in a fight, except for something like judo that depended on skill more than strength.

Turning away and starting down the slope to the house, Bart thought about how he'd called Bill a monster. It had seemed to really upset him. Maybe it was embarrassing to be all overgrown like that. And maybe that was why Bill went around tackling people, to show them how strong he was. Because anyway, Bart concluded, it certainly would be embarrassing to be outsized and to be a weakling at the same time. That would be likely to make anyone feel like a real freak.

But right away he forgot about Bill because there was Miss Matty down by the pile of lumber folding up the tarp she'd pulled off the logs and boards. When he called out to her, she straightened up and called back, "You want to bring down the Styrofoam? It's in the shed."

When he'd joined her with the sections of Styrofoam and a package that he'd found lying on top of them she said, "Now, let's measure off your boards, and length 'em. Oh — do you think you could bring down my saw-horse? By the back door."

The sawhorse was awkward, and rather heavy, but he managed to get it down the slope by turning it end over end along the ground. Miss Matty had started testing her hacksaw on one of the long logs. When he delivered the sawhorse she stopped and said, "I don't know, — the bucksaw might work better. You mind running up again? It's hanging on a nail at the back of the shed." Bart began to wonder if he was going to spend the whole morning running errands and fetching gear. But he reminded himself that it was his project — or anyway he thought it was.

He wasn't so sure of that when he came back with the bucksaw and Miss Matty said, "Now we can get your lumber separate from the rest, and I'll have some idea where I'm at."

Bart hardly dared ask the question that came into his

mind. But he was too anxious to keep still. "Are you —
I mean are we going to start with your shelter?"

She paused and looked at him. "If we start by
lengthening your boards, I'd say we were starting with
your raft, wouldn't you?" she asked him. "No rush about
finishing it, though," she went on. "You've got a way to
go before you've got the hang of the harbor — "

"But couldn't I sort of get the hang of my raft, anyway," he broke in, "by trying it out on the river? I've
figured it all out," he told her. "If I pick the right
tide — "

"Easier said than done," she told him. "You get it off
by a few minutes. you'll find yourself out in the harbor
whether you want to be or not."

He was too worried to more than half listen. It seemed
to him he'd been patient for an awfully long time, and
finally everything was right in his hands, and here she
was acting as if they had all the time in the world, and
they were maybe going to have to put up her shelter —
which might take days — before finishing his raft. And
the awful thing about it was that he was in a pretty poor
position to complain. Without her place to build it, and
without all the help she'd given him, he'd probably never
have a raft at all. It gave him a wild, helpless feeling, as
if he were trapped. But he made himself say, "How long
do you think it'll take to build your shelter?"

"Depends how it goes," she said so calmly that he
could hardly stand it. "Can't do much right now but
114

measure off the ground. One of my neighbors is coming over later with his posthole digger. So let's get on with your boards in the meantime. Then we can tote them down closer to the water — you bring that bundle of glue, by the way?"

Bart thought it was a good sign to have her mention the glue, and his confidence revived a bit. "I guess that's the package that was with the Styrofoam," he said. "Here it is."

At that moment they were both distracted by a hail from the road and there was Bill starting to ride right down the slope. "Leave it up there!" Bart called out to him. The last thing he was interested in just now was his bike, and he'd completely forgotten Bill's watch. But Bill kept on coming down toward them, jouncing on the uneven ground, but keeping the wheel remarkably steady. When he stopped a few yards away from them, Bart said, "Why don't you ride it back up again, where you're so great? And then I won't have to."

Bill said, "Sure!" so cheerfully that Bart felt a little mean. "What're you doing?" Bill asked then.

"Miss Matty's putting up a shelter," Bart told him quickly, because he certainly didn't want Bill knowing about his raft. Miss Matty said hello to Bill, but before she could ask him to join them or something horrible like that Bart said, "You want your watch back now? Or you want to ride around some more?"

It didn't surprise him any that Bill voted to ride. "You

115

going to be here for another hour, maybe?" Bill asked him. He wasn't only looking hopeful, he was looking pretty sure of himself all of a sudden.

Bart had an impulse to spit. But considering everything he just said, "O.K." It had struck him that anything was better than to have Bill hang around and poke his nose into Bart's business. For a minute he watched Bill start to pedal painfully up the slope. Bart wasn't at all sure that he'd be able to even do it, himself, and it was apparent to him that Bill didn't find it easy. He was really struggling, and just barely making it.

"I like his determination," Miss Matty remarked.

Bart said, "He's just showing off," and turned back to the lumber pile.

"Well you did challenge him, you know," she reminded him. "What would you expect him to do?"

"I just expect him to keep showing off," Bart told her stubbornly. "Because all he's got is a lot of muscles and no brains." Before she was able to say anything else that he didn't want to hear he added, "But I know he can't help it, and all. I mean, that's just the way he was made, so I don't hate him, or anything." A second later he thought to say, "After all, I loaned him my bike — twice now!" At once he reached for a really big board and tried to move it as if it didn't actually weigh much of anything.

A few minutes later Miss Matty said, "If you want to start sawing, I'll be marking the boards." As she spoke, she brought up from the pocket of her slacks a

116

coiled, steel tape measure and a really thick, stubby pencil. "What I figure," she said then, "we'll cut the planks a little longer than the Styrofoam. That way, there'll be an overhang, so all you can see, topside, will be wood. The flotation'll be ought of sight, below. Under water, the way I told you." She chuckled. "I don't see how even Jepson could catch us out on that!"

By the time they'd measured and cut all the boards, and then carried them down near to the pier, Bart was pretty sure that at least an hour must have passed. He glanced up at the sun. "I should think Bill would be back by this time," he commented. "I sure hope he hasn't wracked up my bike."

"He looked pretty capable to me," Miss Matty said calmly. "I expect he'll show up around lunchtime, anyway. How's *your* appetite, by the way?"

"Gosh!" Bart said. "I left my lunch in my bike basket. If he loses it — or eats it all — if he eats *one* of my sandwiches — "

Miss Matty said, "Here he comes now."

This time Bart went up to meet him, and the first thing he did was check over his lunch box. After that he dug out Bill's watch and handed it over to him. When Bill had turned it over a couple of times and really examined its condition, he snapped open the case and read the time. "Hey!" he said, "I really made it." He laughed. "You had my watch, but I really timed myself. How do you like that?" He was looking as if he thought he was a genius, which was practically pathetic in Bart's

117

opinion, so he only said, "So what d'you need a watch for?" Immediately Bill stuffed it into his pocket, and said, "I just like it — and besides it's mine!"

Bart picked up his bike, looked it over, rang the bell, and said, "I guess it's time to go home for lunch," like a loud hint.

Bill got it, too. But just before moving away he said, "I guess you'll really trust me after this."

"Oh, sure," Bart told him, as nicely as possible. "Only not all the time!" he felt the need to add because he didn't want Bill getting the idea he could take Bart's bike any old time he wanted to. "See you around," he called after him. It satisfied himself as sounding pretty friendly without being too darned enthusiastic.

When he joined Miss Matty again she really smiled at him, so he thought she was satisfied with him, too. "Tell you what," she said then, "when my neighbor gets over here with his posthole digger, I'll work along with him, and you can start in gluing your boards. Why don't you read those directions while you're eating your lunch?"

Bart never read the directions for anything. But sometimes he wished he had, afterward. Anyway he was really eager to study the printed sheet that had come with the package of glue. *Gosh,* he was thinking, *I might get the whole raft built this afternoon!*

12

Bart woke up earlier than usual on Sunday morning, and he got out of bed at once. While he pulled on his clothes he thought about his raft the way he had left it the day before, practically finished. He'd studied the directions for gluing and really followed them, and he was sure that nothing on land or sea could pry his boards loose from the Styrofoam. He was willing to bet that they were bonded together for good.

Miss Matty had let him use her tarpaulin to cover up his raft for the night. Just before spreading it and tucking it under all around, he had stood stock still and simply looked for a number of minutes at the result of his labors, and the realization of his dream. It was beautiful! The new wood was clean and light, and it was nicely grained. The boards really matched, like the planking on a ship's deck. Even without a whole lot of planing and sanding, they were just about perfect. His imagination moved on to the time when the wood might darken, and get weathered. But he figured that it would still be beautiful. He imagined it getting smoother and smoother like a fine-grained piece of driftwood worn soft by salt water and sand. He could almost feel its polished surface against his bare feet.

The raft was really finished, except for mounting the blocks he'd cut out to carry the oarlocks. He planned to get them on this morning, and by the time Miss Matty got back from church the raft would be ready for a trial run. He'd checked the tide. It would turn about noon, and that was exactly right. Twelve-forty-five to be exact. If they shoved off about twelve, they could make a nice run and return with the incoming tide a little less than an hour later. Miss Matty hadn't really promised to make the run, but she hadn't refused, either. And it seemed to him that she got a pretty interested look on her face when he mentioned the subject.

He was so early that his mother hadn't even got down yet, and he had the kitchen to himself. He considered trying to fry a couple of eggs and some bacon, but he settled for raiding the bread box, eating five biscuits covered with butter and jam, and then drinking three glasses of milk. He decided against making himself a lunch. He might get back in time to eat at home, anyway. If it came to the worst, he guessed Miss Matty would feed him. Meantime he was in no mood to waste a lot of time making sandwiches. He scrawled on his mother's shopping list, "Back for dinner," which was a truthful possibility, at least.

The town was so quiet, and the streets so empty, that

he resisted the impulse to burst into song. Generally he hated Sundays. Everything seemed to grind to a halt and nothing the least bit interesting ever happened. But this morning it struck him as sort of nice. Peaceful! And there was no one at all around to interfere with his plans. As he rode on toward the river he began to feel as if he had the world to himself. And any minute now he was going to have the river to himself.

For a while it was just the way he imagined it. Apparently Miss Matty wasn't up yet either and he was entirely alone. Uncovering his raft, and then folding the tarp into the neatest bundle he could make, he paused a couple of times to look out across the marsh grass and the river, and dream. It was all his — Miss Matty's house, and the pier, and the catboat. He lived here, and everything belonged to him. How about the cats, though? There were a couple of them already sharpening their claws on the tall posts, trying them out. Now that the posts were properly sunk they looked just about the right height. And the cats acted as if they knew exactly what they were for. As soon as the roof went on, Bart guessed the cats would be trying it out, too. But thinking about them, he had another idea. Suppose he were to take some of them with him on his raft? Probably an island would be about the safest place in the world for them. He bet Miss Matty would be delighted if he could reduce her cat population and move them to such an ideal location. No one to chase them, nothing to harm them — it would be perfect! And

121

maybe they'd learn to do their own fishing in the pools left by the receding tides. It struck him as one of his best dreams. And it was so practical, too! He might just take a couple of cats the first time, and then if he found exactly the island he was looking for, he could come back for some more. He imagined himself running a regular cat ferry, and it made him laugh. Catboat, catfish, cat ferry. Of course there were catastrophes, too, he thought next. But he dismissed that idea at once. Right now he didn't feel like worrying, for a change.

Before attaching the two blocks he wondered which might be considered the prow, and which the stern, on a raft. Both ends were the same. Still, canoes were also shaped the same way at either end. At least that's the way they looked. So he guessed it was all right. In one way he liked his raft to be unique and different from anything else. At the same time he didn't want it to be a freak sort of a craft. He finally concluded that it was pretty convenient the way it was, and if a person wanted to he could mount an oar at either end. That way he could probably start going in the opposite direction without even turning the raft around. Just the same, for the time being he settled for mounting both blocks at the same end.

The sun was a good bit higher, and feeling really warm when Bart stepped back and looked at his raft completed, with blocks and oarlocks in place. After a bit he picked up one end and hefted the weight. Even with the light, Styrofoam underpinning it weighed quite a lot. Well, it was rugged, and that's the way he wanted it. And he thought he could get it into the water, and then out again when the time came. A canoe might be lighter, but a dory had to be a lot heavier and he'd beached a couple of dories when he was at camp.

He lifted it again, and rocked and swiveled it a little so that when he dropped it, he'd moved it a trifle closer to the water. He glanced at the sun, and then he looked up toward the house. There was smoke coming out of the kitchen chimney now. Apparently Miss Matty was up, and cooking breakfast on her ancient coal stove. She was very likely cooking fish and liver and stuff, too. Remembering all those smells, he made a face. He certainly was glad he didn't have to eat in the middle of all that. He thought it would ruin his appetite even if he was pretty hungry. Come to think of it, he was beginning to feel a little hungry right now. Maybe he ought to have taken the time to pack a lunch, after all. He squinted at the sun again and tried to guess what time it might be.

Just then the door opened and Miss Matty stepped outside, although he hardly recognized her, all dressed up the way she was. She was even wearing white gloves, he realized, when she briefly waved at him before starting up toward the shed. Bart groaned. Here she was only starting off to church! It would be an hour anyway before she could possibly get back, and he had absolutely nothing left to do, on top of not even having anything to eat. He heard the jeep start, and then he watched it

123

jolt up the slope and off down the road, with Miss Matty's dress-up hat bobbing above the steering wheel.

Now he had the whole place to himself for a fact — and it didn't suit him at all. An hour, he told himself again. At least an hour. How could things be so impossible? He thought about his mother talking about patience. It was one of her favorite subjects. "You must learn to be patient," she frequently said. There were a lot of things he wanted to learn but patience wasn't one of them. In fact he hated the idea. The way he looked at it, everything ought to be quick — quick and alive! And if he, Bart, were arranging the world, that's the way it would be. Things would keep happening, and you wouldn't ever have to sit around waiting for them to happen. He threw up his hands to heaven, and then he brought them down to clutch his own head. "An hour!" he said desperately again. It was so awful that he had to do something or lose his mind.

He decided to go out on the pier where he could really look at the water. There was nothing slow about the river, anyway. It didn't have to wait for anything, and maybe that was one reason he liked it so much. It kept moving all the time, and pretty fast, too. Right now it seemed to be racing, downward to the sea. He wondered if it moved faster just before the tide turned. There was still quite a lot he had to learn about the river, and the tides, and the harbor. But he wasn't learning anything just standing around here waiting. He kicked a pebble off the pier and turned back towards
124

his raft. It occurred to him that instead of stalling around he might get his raft moved even closer to the river. If he could get it really jockeyed into position then it should be fairly easy to slide it into the water later on. He set himself to accomplishing that.

By lifting it, and rocking it, and edging it along the ground he got it right onto the high, grassy bank of the river. It wouldn't take much more than a nudge to land it in the water from here. He went back after an oar, and when he'd brought it down beside the raft there was nothing left to do. Everything was in readiness for the trial run as soon as Miss Matty got back, whenever that might be. He wished he had a watch. If he had a watch like Bill's he could set the alarm and take a nap, for example. He wouldn't have to waste any time and he wouldn't have to miss anything, either. Or if he had a portable TV like Alec was going to get. That would be the greatest! He began to imagine himself just sitting here on the bank of the river and watching all the shows from New York and Hollywood and all over. He imagined the screen being as big as the screen at a drive-in movie. It was huge! It blotted out the sky. It covered the whole landscape. At that point he said, "Heck!" and sat down hard. There wasn't anything on any TV or anywhere else that he'd rather look at than the Salt River. Suppose he had that portable TV with a screen as big as all outdoors? And then suppose he couldn't turn it off when he wanted to? There he'd be forever and ever like someone under an evil spell. Just the idea

125

of it made him shudder. Maybe after all he ought to stretch out and take a little nap.

In the next minute he heard a shout and looked up to see Bill coming down from the road. He was approaching by leaps and bounds across the uneven ground. Bart's immediate impulse was to hide his raft, or somehow conceal it. But that was out of the question. If he'd brought the tarp along with him, which of course he hadn't, there still wouldn't be time to unfold and use it. He was really caught, unless he could manage to persuade Bill that the raft was something Miss Matty was building — like a diving float, or a replacement for her old pier.

Bill was being so energetic and looking so darned cheerful that Bart figured he didn't need any encouragement so he just nodded at him in a bored sort of way without even saying hello. Bill didn't seem to notice the omission and he was apparently more than ready to do all the talking himself. He said it was a great day and it really made you feel good even if you didn't have much of anything to do. He said it would be a perfect day for a real outing, like with a picnic lunch and all, and he certainly wished he had a bike, too, and then they could go to the beach or someplace. "No kidding," he said then. "I mean, I'm not hinting or anything," Bart just nodded again. "My father would get me a bike," Bill said next, "only I guess he worries about me. I guess he thinks I might get killed or something."

Bart broke his silence to say, "You could, all right."
126

It came out sounding a lot more grim than he'd intended and he wasn't surprised to have Bill give him a startled look, and then change the subject.

"That looks like a new float," he remarked. Bart sat a little straighter. This was exactly what he'd been hoping for, that Bill would come to his own conclusions without Bart having to make up any stories, or really say anything at all. "Did you help build it?" he asked. Bart nodded. "When're you going to launch it?" was Bill's next question.

"Oh, I don't know," Bart said vaguely. "I guess that's up to Miss Matty."

"Hey!" Bill said, "why don't we surprise her? Why don't we put it in the water for her right now?" He made a clumsy sort of lunge at the raft as if he expected to pick it up in one hoist. And then, because he was clumsy, or because he was stronger than he realized, he actually overturned it, and in the next instant it had flipped over the bank and landed in the river. Bart was horrified.

The bank of the river was just high enough to put him out of easy reach of the water. What he needed was a good, long boat hook, but he reached for the only thing he had, which was his oar. He managed to get it to the downstream end of the raft, and then he tried to hold it there, like a brake. But he was in an awkward position, and it was impossible to bring much strength to bear at that distance. His raft was being drawn toward the center of the current and its greatest speed. In another min-

127

ute it would be swept from his reach altogether. Clutching the oar in both hands now, he made a desperate, flying leap from the bank.

The raft swung sidewise when he hit it, and then it rocked wildly. So much water splashed over him that he wasn't sure he hadn't capsized already. But at least he'd gauged well and landed on the raft and not in the river. After a bit he realized that the raft was beginning to steady itself. The knowledge gave him a brief, proud satisfaction. It was just as stable as he'd always thought it would be! He had another problem, though. He'd been sucked into midstream now and was really moving with the tide.

He was dimly aware of Bill chattering at him from the bank, but he was much too concerned with his own situation to pay much attention. What he needed to do first was to position the oar and get it working, and gave himself some control. Without it he was as helpless as a chip on the water, totally at the mercy of the current which seemed to move faster and faster. Turning to place the oar at the stern, he took a quick backward look and was startled to see how far he had drifted already. Bill was shouting after him now, but only his voice and not his words arrived.

Bart applied himself to the oar. Then he really leaned on it. He was giving it all his strength and yet he only succeeded in nosing the raft slightly against the tide. The raft, not turned but only the least bit angled, crabwise, was moving at the same, unchecked speed. Any hope of
128

really steering, and finally getting to shore, began to fade from his mind. He was caught in the full, running tide and he suspected that if he were twice as strong he'd still be no match for it. For the first time he faced the possibility that his father might be right about the dangers of a tidal river.

Just before he was swept around a bend, Bart looked back once more. Bill was still standing there on the bank, a very small figure now, outlined against the sky. He wasn't waving, and Bart was sure that he wasn't calling after him any longer. He was just standing there, very still, and all by himself. It came to Bart that what he looked was lonely. He looked like about the loneliest person in the world. In a clutch of something like panic Bart wondered if he would ever see him again.

13

Beyond the bend, which shut off all view of Miss Matty's house and the bank where Bill stood, Bart discovered that the river widened and there were flat sandy shoals at either side. A slight hope revived in him. The thing to do was to take advantage of one of the river's many curves. If he put all his strength to the oar, in the direction that the river swung, between his effort and the thrust of the current, the raft should be driven to shore. Once landed he would simply wait for the turn of the tide and ride it back up the river. He had a swift, momentary vision of himself gliding smoothly, effortlessly back to Miss Matty's pier.

He was able to relax a little and look around him. There was the house where the Doberman lived, and on the opposite shore, much closer, a cabin he'd never noticed before. It was nestled amongst the trees, and somewhat screened from the water by shrubbery. It might be someone's shooting box with the shrubs making a duckblind. Whatever it was, it appealed to him. It was a neat

130

size, in the first place. It struck him as just his size, and a place he'd like to move into. There it was right on the river, and still it had a hidden, secret sort of look about it. Apparently it was unoccupied, though he figured a person could live there without being noticed, if he wanted to.

Further along, on the same shore, there was a really big place. The house was dark-stained wood with long, overhanging roofs and balconies from the second-story windows. It looked like a ski lodge you might see in the mountains, and was almost big enough to be a small hotel. It wasn't Bart's size at all, but he had to admire it. It looked romantic, even shuttered up the way it was. In the summer, with people on the balconies, and strolling around on the sweeping lawns, he imagined it would be like a place in a movie. Maybe the little cabin belonged to it. It might be the boat house, or something like that, since both places were empty. He imagined the owners letting him use the little cabin. They might even sell it to him, and for next to nothing, since they had so much other space all to themselves and probably more money than they knew what to do with.

He saw that another curve was coming up ahead, but it wasn't the really sharp one he was looking for. He could easily see around it, so he decided against trying to make a landing there. The ideal place would be a switchback sort of a bend, and preferably with the river narrowing beyond it. He went back to scanning the shores at either side. It was all just the way he had imag-

131

ined it, with something different and interesting appearing all the time. If he didn't have anything to worry about, he could really enjoy it. If he already had his sail, for example, he could sit back and give himself up to the pure pleasure of the trip. That's the way it would be if he'd planned the run the way he'd intended to do. Just the same he didn't have a moment's regret about choosing to grab the raft and go with it. It was the only thing he could possibly have done, under the circumstances. You couldn't even call it a choice! His raft was being swept away and out of his life forever. He'd jumped on sheer impulse, and in desperation — and he would do it again. And with any luck, he told himself, with any luck at all he could surely manage to land it long before he got to the harbor.

He remembered Miss Matty saying that he could find himself out in the harbor whether he wanted to be there or not. He began to wonder how much longer the river might be. Maybe he'd meet someone along the shore, or better still out in a boat. He hadn't seen a soul since he last looked back at Bill. Everything was very quiet and no one seemed to be around. Well, it was early in the season, and it was Sunday, too. It was exactly what he'd expected of a Sunday, and right now he didn't feel like calling it peaceful. He wouldn't call it boring, either. What he felt was anxious and uneasy. In fact he'd be pretty worried if he broke down and gave in to it. He didn't have his sail; the current was a lot stronger than he was; and there was no hope of the tide turning

132

for quite some time. He thought of Bill with a surge of anger. It was all his fault! It was just the kind of thing he would do with all his muscles and no brains.

Maybe by this time Bill was off and away on Bart's bike. He might have just been waiting there on the bank until Bart got out of sight — and maybe for good and all. The way Bart was beginning to feel, he wouldn't be at all surprised if he were swept out to sea and never got back again. He'd told himself that Bill looked lonely, but it was he, Bart, who was the lonely one. He guessed that was what he had actually meant, and now he was facing it. He guessed it was himself who was about the loneliest person in the world, riding a runaway raft on a current he couldn't control. He might never see Bill again, or anybody else.

By now he was so overcome by his own helplessness, and danger, that he felt weak. Actually, he felt faint, too, and as if he were going to be sick. He leaned against the oar blocks and when he'd steadied himself a bit, he reached out to scoop up some water and slosh it over his head and face. The shock of the cold salt water was refreshing and he began to feel less faint. But his stomach didn't feel any better. A minute or so later it occurred to him that he was empty. His stomach was gnawing with hunger and he figured that must be at least partly why he felt so weak. But there was absolutely nothing he could do about it. It was only one more hopeless problem in his whole hopeless situation. He was quite sure he'd heard somewhere, or read, that if a person were starving he could prolong life a while, at least, if he had some water to drink. But all he had was salt water.

He'd swept around a number of bends without managing to even graze the further shore. The river didn't seem to narrow, and now it struck him that the houses were becoming more numerous. Right now he was passing a regular little colony of houses and piers. So perhaps he was approaching the harbor which he was sure was more thickly settled. The next curve of the river was obscured by an unexpected stand of trees.

When he'd been carried past the trees and into the open again he was surprised to see that a bridge spanned the river at some distance ahead. Beyond that, he felt sure, was the harbor, although he could only see the open sky above it. He set his hopes on the bridge and tightened his grip on the oar, while a sudden envy of Bill ran through him. Bill was probably strong enough to really control the raft. At this moment Bart would have given every brain in his head in exchange for Bill's muscles.

He focused all his attention on the bridge. It wasn't very high, and if he stood up and stretched he thought it might even be possible to get hold of a strut or some part of the understructure. Then if he could keep his feet on the raft, he might pull himself, hand over hand, to where the bridge joined the dry land. But suppose he lost his raft in the process? He was scared, and he had good reason to be. He was in real danger. And still he wasn't willing to give up his raft. He told himself that it

135

shouldn't be necessary. He ought to be able to get ashore *with* it. Besides, if it got away from him, where would he be left? He imagined himself hanging by his hands from the bridge, out of sight even if there were anyone around to see him. There might or might not be any possible handholds with which to swing himself to the end of the bridge. In any case, the bridge was very long because the river, at this point, was very wide. His strength might wholly give out before he ever made it. Or he might actually faint, with exhaustion and hunger.

He was close enough now to really study the underside of the bridge. He was dimly aware of something slightly familiar about it, or about the whole scene. But he couldn't really think about it at the moment. For one thing, he had to stand up — quickly, but without rocking the raft. He got to his knees, and was about to spring to his feet, when the raft really went out of control. It whirled around, briefly straightened, and was immediately caught in another spin.

Now he knew why the scene was familiar. Beneath the bridge the river was a mass of whirlpools, and just at the other side, the water really boiled. He'd been brought here a long time ago because his uncle wanted to watch some kayak races. Bart had been very young, and he had really forgotten about it. He certainly hadn't remembered — if he had even known at the time — that the setting was the Salt River. But he was suddenly seeing it all as if it had happened yesterday. The men were like parts of the narrow little boats. It was as if the can-

136

vas decking was an extension of their clothes, it came up so tight around their waists. It seemed to hold them into the kayaks, and at the same time to prevent any water from getting in with them when they overturned. He remembered that they had kept overturning, whether by accident or on purpose. Boat and man together would roll, disappear under the water, and then roll back upright again. Now he was vividly remembering his fascination and his fear. He had been excited and at the same time terrified by the churning white water, and the tiny boats bucking and rolling and disappearing into the river. Even though the men bobbed upright again, he still expected, every time, that they would be gone for good. He was pretty sure he had cried, in terror at something so strange and so incomprehensible. He was a lot bigger now, and he was almost as frightened.

If only the whirlpools would cast him ashore! They were certainly powerful. His rugged raft spun like a saucer. But the motion was almost entirely circular, and only the tug of the tide pulled him out of one revolution and sent him into another. He wasn't any longer even trying to use the oar.

When he'd been tossed out from under the bridge, and into the white water, he looked up, and ahead. He saw what he had feared he would see. It was still at some distance, but there was nothing any longer between himself and the harbor.

Desperately he scanned the shores. There were plenty of houses, but there were no people around. He supposed

137

they were all inside eating their Sunday dinners. He looked again toward the mouth of the river. There seemed to be quite a group of buildings there, as he had expected there would be. They were his last hope, and in the intensity of his fear and his concentration, he broke out in a cold sweat. He was more than hoping, he was trying to *will* into existence someone who could rescue him before he was tumbled, with the tumbling tide, into the wide harbor and the open sea beyond.

As he came closer to the river's mouth he could see that the buildings at one side were the sheds of a commercial enterprise. When he was able to read the signs he saw that boats and outboard motors were for hire there. But it all had a closed look. Too early in the season again? A couple of ramps had been built out into the water, for launching boats, maybe, or for the take-off for water-skiing. He made a final, fierce effort to head the raft in their direction. But here the tide seemed to be even swifter, and his efforts even more futile.

Why didn't the tide turn? He thought it must be nearly time. And surely that would reverse him, and send him back upstream. But he was rushing into the harbor, and now he became aware of a strong offshore wind at his back. He thought about Miss Matty talking about shifty winds and unaccountable tides. So maybe he was caught in both? The harbor looked very large, and the open sea appeared to him to be as endless as the sky.

138

14

THE HARBOR WAS FORMED by a point of land, like a long, curved sandbar that was scattered with dunes and dune-grass. Toward the open end, between the shore and the outer beach, there were mussel beds. When the tide was wholly out, they were uncovered, and stood out like a stretch of exposed mud flats, almost like dry land, in the middle of the harbor.

Bart realized that the wind, and the tide that was still receding, were driving the raft toward the mussel beds. They weren't yet entirely uncovered, but he knew that the water there would be extremely shallow already, and perhaps by the time he reached them he would go aground. Ground, in any stable sense, wasn't the word for that stretch. It was a deep, soft slime or ooze that a person couldn't possibly walk on. But at least it ought to halt the raft, and hold it until the tide returned. He glanced at the sun. It was just about overhead. He would have expected the time to be well past noon. It certainly seemed as if he'd been riding the raft for an awfully long time. But time was a funny thing. It depended on what you were doing with it. He realized now, with dismay, that it might have been less than an hour ago that his raft had gone over the bank, and he had jumped after it. In that case, total low tide might be close to another hour away.

Meantime he was moving a lot faster than he wished he were. And now he thought of another problem. Any craft that had a keel, almost any boat really, would be certain to strand on a shoal. But his raft was flat-bottomed, and it drew so little water that it might pass right through a shallow where anything else would be arrested. Even a few inches of water might allow it to ride over the flats. For the first time he seriously considered abandoning his raft and striking out to swim to shore. Someone might pick up the raft. Or, unweighted and left to the waves and wind, it might bring up on the outer beach. He glanced back.

He had come quite a way, although it was a distance that he believed he could swim, normally. But right now he was feeling far from normal. The sun was surprisingly hot and if he wasn't burned, he was certainly parched. His throat was so dry it hurt to swallow, and he wasn't at all sure he could shout if he had to. Worse than his thirst, though, was his hunger and the weak way it made him feel. Then, he reasoned that he'd be swimming against the tide, and he'd have the wind in his face. He glanced back once more, and this time the distance looked impossible to him.

The clear sandy bottom was darkening, and muddying up. He was nearing the mussel beds. They made him think of turtles, and eels, and even sharks, though he'd never actually heard of a shark off these shores. But once on the beach he had seen a dead turtle that was a lot bigger than he was. He was told it weighed four hundred pounds. He began to think that maybe, after all, he'd just as soon not strand on the mud flats. A few minutes later, with a sense of some relief, he found himself passing over them. There was perhaps a foot of water between him and the black, slimy bottom.

Beyond the flats, the water deepened abruptly. But it was hard to guess how deep it might be because something was changing about the tide, too, and he could no longer see the bottom. It seemed as though, approaching the tip of the sand spit, the tide accelerated. Close to the very tip, something more complicated than that was going on. Bart wondered if this was a rip tide, as if somehow in the meeting of the harbor with the outer sea a turmoil was set up in the opposing currents. And it they were in conflict, then which one was likely to win? Would he be swept around the point? Or could he possibly be caught in the middle and tossed endlessly in the commotion? He didn't even know what to hope for, or which was the more frightening fate. But he wasn't given much time to ponder it.

Apparently he was going to be caught in the middle. He was pitching and rocking in the churn of the water, but he didn't seem to be progressing either forward or back. It reminded him of the whirlpools under the bridge. But this was worse, and more alarming. He thought briefly of those men in the kayaks. They had to be awfully strong! But in this situation, he doubted if they could do a thing. He suspected that even a sail wouldn't help much here. What was needed was a motor, and a really powerful one.

He'd never been seasick in his life, and he would have sworn that he never could be. But the ceaseless rolling boil of this water was making him feel very queasy. Yet how could he possibly be sick with nothing in his stomach to throw up? Like an answer to his question a terrible, dry heave seemed to overturn his stomach. Maybe something had torn loose and his stomach itself was coming up? In pain, and fear, and helpless frustration he doubled up and sobbed. It was too much. It was more than anyone could be expected to stand. And since he was obviously doomed, why didn't he die and be done with it?

He couldn't possibly have said how long he huddled there, shaking in misery, before something changed again. The sea began to quiet, and the raft started to steady. Shortly after that a single current seemed to take over, to straighten and then drive the raft. It was as though the sea's conflict had ended, and one clear tide had prevailed. Helped on by the wind, which was very strong here at the point, Bart was being carried around the sand spit and into the open sea.

He figured that the tide had halted, but hadn't yet
142

quite turned. The sudden calm must mark the end of the outgoing tide and the beginning of the lull that preceded the incoming one. Except for the stir of the wind, the sea was remarkably still. Beginning to recover a little and look around him, Bart decided that the ocean had paused, and was resting. It began to seem to him as though it were waiting, when the stillness went on and on. Maybe it had to gather its strength in order to hurl its spent waters back at the land again? He found himself thinking of the sea as if it were alive, a living presence, like an enormous animal that leapt and ran and roared, and then lay down to rest in order to leap again.

Now that his stomach had stabilized, what he chiefly felt was exhaustion. In fact he felt limp with fatigue. Nothing appealed to him more at this moment than simply going to sleep, and for a second he closed his eyes. He discovered that it hurt. Whether from the sting of the salt water, or because his eyeballs were sunburned, they smarted. It was almost as if there were sand under his lids that gritted against his eyes, and he quickly opened them again. In any case it might be dangerous to allow himself to fall asleep. The worst thing a person could do in the snow, he knew, was to give up and let himself go to sleep. And perhaps it was just as hazardous to anyone adrift on the sea.

He propped himself up a little straighter. He was still holding on to the oar in an automatic sort of way, and now he tried to take a firmer grip. Maybe, in this relative calm, he could even manage to steer. But the wind hadn't subsided, and it was still coming off the shore, at his back, and sending him constantly further from land. Was he destined to be lost at sea? Or might he be cast on some island, after all? He struggled weakly, and really from habit, to imagine an island. He didn't want it to be a desert island. He wanted someone to be living there, and with all sorts of supplies — particularly water and food! First he would drink all the water he could hold, and then he would start to eat. He would eat, and eat, and eat — and then he would lie down and sleep.

Just the thought of sleeping nearly overcame him. He absolutely had to stay awake! Maybe it would help if he moved around a bit? He might try standing up. Using the oar for support, he got cautiously to his feet. In the next minute he was charged with a burst of confidence and hope that was like the miraculous return of his strength. It was a ship! Out there, close to the horizon, was the dark bulk of a ship.

Still standing, he started to really labor the oar. And now it seemed to be having some effect. He had not only regained his normal strength, it was as if he had been given some extra strength. He felt like Bill, and better. He felt as if he could do anything — and he was going out to that ship! In confidence, and joy he raised his eyes again to the distant line where ocean and sky came together. It was somewhat short of the horizon that the ship had stood. He looked quickly, anxiously, to the left and then to the right. He scanned the whole expanse of the sea. What had become of the ship? Could it
144

possibly have steamed out of sight? But only minutes had passed! He looked and looked, and strained to look even farther. There was nothing to be seen but the unbroken breadth of water and sky. As far as his sight could range there was only the uninhabited ocean, and the sky that was blank as an unused slate.

Bart's hope collapsed and his strength ebbed out of him like a spent tide. Maybe he was losing his mind. Maybe he was delirious. The ship might have been a mirage, such as men lost on the desert saw when their minds were deranged by hunger and thirst, and deluded by desperate hope. In exhaustion and despair he dropped back to huddle on the floor of the raft, and wedging himself against the idle oar, he gave in to the temptation to sleep.

When he was finally waked by a noise nearby, his first impression was that the day had changed. He looked in alarm toward the sun. It must be late afternoon, and his imagination raced on to picture the oncoming night. But the noise that had wakened him was louder, closer again, and this time he realized that it came from overhead.

The small plane must have been circling him, and now the wings dipped as if in salute, or recognition. Bart had barely started to wave in return when the plane reversed direction and flew back toward the land. He was fully awake by now and he began to speculate on what it meant. Either the pilot had been sent to case his possible position, or had come upon him during a routine flight. In either case, his dilemma was now known, and his location in the water, and presumably a boat would be sent to his rescue.

A new sort of tiredness was taking him over now. He felt weary in a relaxed kind of way, as though his struggle were at an end, and his safety were assured. He pushed at the oar idly, in the confidence that it no longer mattered whether it worked or not. He was even able to think about his thirst and his hunger, and what he began to imagine was a huge pitcher of milk.

15

Bart heard the boat approaching and when he had turned sufficiently to look back, he saw it. But it was a number of minutes before he could positively identify it as belonging to the Coast Guard station. He stood up and waved wildly. Without giving any other indication of having seen him, the captain veered slightly from his course and headed directly for Bart. The boat was almost close enough to run down the raft before Bart recognized Miss Matty on deck, and then his brother, Alec, beside her.

Neither one of them was smiling and only Miss Matty gave Bart a brief wave. It seemed to him they ought to be delighted to see him. He'd never in his life been so glad to see anyone. He was even glad to see Alec. He guessed he honestly hadn't expected to ever see anyone again. He'd seriously expected to die, alone, in the appalling lonely vastness of the sea.

The captain reversed, and then brought the boat to a position broadside of Bart's raft and close enough for a line to reach. When the line had been released and shot to Bart, there was a life preserver fastened to the end of it. Bart caught it, a little awkwardly, and then he dropped the life preserver over one of the oar blocks, like a ring in a game of ring toss. He had supposed they were planning to tow him, raft and all, but the captain was apparently dissatisfied with Bart's maneuver, and he presently cast him a second, looped line. "You attach that one to the raft," he called down, "and we'll bring you aboard with the doughnut." It was an order.

The rescue line seemed to work on a windlass and once Bart had secured the tow rope to the raft, he found himself being reeled in like a hooked fish. Alec gave him a hoist up over the side, and there he was safe aboard.

For a minute he just stood there, weak with relief and unable to do anything but smile foolishly. Then he managed to say what was uppermost in his mind. "I didn't think anyone would ever find me. Gosh, I was scared!"

"You certainly scared us," Miss Matty told him severely.

"But I didn't mean to," Bart said hoarsely, his voice coming out like a croak.

"That's what your buddy told us," Alec put in. "He said it was all his fault."

"You mean Bill?" Bart was surprised.

"If it wasn't for Bill," Miss Batty said, "you never would have been found. No one would have known where you were. We wouldn't have had the least idea what happened."

148

Before he could say anything more Bert had to ask for a drink of water. It was Alec who went into the little cabin and came out with a canteen. "Don't drink too much right away," he advised. "Sort of swish it around in your mouth and just swallow a little."

It sounded sensible but what impressed Bart the most was that Alec seemed so concerned. He acted as if he cared, and he was looking very serious and being very quiet. He wasn't being any way that Bart had ever seen him before. It was as if he were suddenly all grown up. And that made Bart think about his parents. "Does Pop — ?" he started to ask.

Miss Matty broke in to say, "When Bill told me what had happened, I phoned your family. But I got Alec — and here we are."

Bart kept looking at his brother. "Does Pop know, though?" he asked him now. The possibility really upset him, athough he would have thought nothing else could upset him after all he'd been through.

"I didn't say anything," Alec told him. "What d'you think I am, a rat? Anyway, Mom would have had a stroke."

The captain had swung the boat around and they were moving quite rapidly. Bart wanted to thank Alec, or somehow tell him how grateful he was. But nothing he could think of to say seemed the least bit adequate. He leaned against the railing, and then he slumped down to sit on the deck. "I'll be glad to get on land," he said weakly. "I mean, something that doesn't move." He glanced at

149

Miss Matty. "Maybe Pop was right all the time — " he suggested. "About the Salt River, and all." He wanted to say some more about how rough it had been. He wanted to tell them about the whirlpools, and the rip tide, and how scared he had been, and how sick he had felt, and how he had never expected to survive. But Miss Matty spoke up.

"Nothing wrong with the river!" she said. "Only you've got to understand it — the way I've been telling you all along. You live with the tides, you've got to know the tides. And that goes twice for a tidal river. It's got its own laws, and a person needs to learn 'em!"

"I meant to," Bart told her. "I was waiting for you to get back and — "

"Maybe you should have just let the raft go," she broke in again. "That ever occur to you?"

"But, gosh!" Bart started to protest, and then Alec picked it up.

"You can understand that, though," he said, appealing to Miss Matty. "Your car, or your bike, or your boat — you can't just let them get away from you. You've got to try to hang onto 'em. And Bart made the raft! It was all his! And he'd only just finished it. He hadn't even tried it out." He was saying everything that Bart wanted to say. And then he said something more. "Anyway, it was gutsy," he said. "You've got to give him credit for that." Bart practically felt like hugging him, but he still couldn't think of anything to say.

150

"Nobody's criticizing his courage," Miss Matty allowed.

Alec suddenly moved off toward the stern of the boat. Maybe he was feeling embarrassed, too? Bart watched him go to lean against the railing and stare down at the following raft. When he came back it struck Bart that he was looking more like himself. "Know what?" he asked Bart. "You ought to rig that for sailing. You put on enough canvas, you could really travel! Flat on the water, no wind resistance, and pretty light — with a real spread of sail it would be like a Sunfish, only better."

"That's what I figured, too," Bart told him. "That's what I was going to do next."

Through the railing he could see that they were close to the outer beach, and the spit of sand. He was sure the rip tide was no longer a problem. In any case, a boat this size could really ride it out. He guessed the mussel beds would be well under water by now, too. But there was something troubling his mind. The next thing he knew they would be inside the harbor, and then back on shore, and then headed home. He stood up. "About Pop — " he began anxiously. He hated to bring it up, about his secrecy and all, but he didn't seem to have much choice. "I didn't plan on telling Pop about my raft," he said.

Alec's reaction was, *"No kidding."* It sounded like his old superior, sarcastic style, and for a second Bart felt hurt, all over again. But then he realized that his brother was looking amused. At least his eyes were. It came to

151

Bart that Alec just couldn't resist being funny, and all of a sudden Bart was able to laugh. "I guess that was obvious all right," he admitted.

"So how about leveling with me," Alec said next. "What did you really have in mind? Shoving off and finding a desert island, or something like that?"

Bart hesitated. His brother sounded perfectly serious but Bart still wasn't sure he could totally trust him. He settled for asking, "Why do you say that?"

Alec shrugged. "It's not unheard of. You aren't exactly the only person who's ever thought of it, you know."

"Did you ever think of it, for instance?" Bart asked.

Now it was Alec who hesitated. He looked away, and then he looked back at Bart again. "When Pop's giving me a really hard time, and Mom's so busy spoiling you that she hardly even knows I exist — "

"Hey!" Bart broke in, "you figure Mom really — well *favors* me, or something? Is that what you think?" He was astonished, and he felt sort of indignant, too. At the same time there was a part of him that was pretty pleased with the idea.

Alec gave him a searching look, and Bart was afraid he was going to get sarcastic again, or just clam up. But then his brother said, "You're the baby — remember? I wish I had a dime for every time Mom says, 'But Bart's younger than you.' I wish — "

Bart broke in with, "I wish I had a nickel — a mere nickel — for every time she says, 'But Alec's older than you.' "

152

Miss Matty had been up talking with the captain and just now she came back to ask Alec, "Did we leave the jeep at the town pier? I was so addled and so upset that I can't remember for sure."

"That's right," Alec told her. "And my car — I mean my family's car — is at your place." When he looked ahead, Bart turned to look with him. They were close to land.

"I guess I upset everyone," Bart felt the need to say. "But most of all me."

"Can we count on that?" Miss Matty asked him. He knew what she meant, and it made him feel foolish. But before he could come up with anything she said, "You certainly upset poor Bill. I don't think he'll ever be the same again."

Bart was inspired with a flash of humor. "Can we count on that, Miss Matty?" he said. Alec laughed, and Bart's spirits shot up. He didn't believe he'd ever in his life before made Alec laugh in appreciation and not in ridicule. But Miss Matty was looking serious.

"If you're referring to the cats," she said, "I left Bill sitting on my pier trying to catch some fish for them. He wanted to do something and I thought that might calm him down. And he's got your bike right beside him," she added, "where he can keep an eye on it for you." With that she moved off to the forward rail and started scanning the shore.

"She's all right," Alec said, "you know that?" Bart just nodded. He was glad that Miss Matty had won Alec's

153

approval, but half his mind was occupied with considering that maybe Bill was all right, too. He guessed Bill was really worried about him. He could see him again standing there on the bank of the river watching Bart out of sight. All at once Bart's imagination started to work again. He began to imagine that he was telling Bill all about it, about sweeping down the river, out of all control, and then getting sucked into those whirlpools, and then being caught in the rip tide, and then being cast into the open ocean and sighting that ghost ship or whatever it was. Bill would be impressed, all right. Bart could imagine him hanging on his every word.

He was jolted back to the present by Alec saying, "Know what I think?" He yawned, and stretched, before saying, "I think you ought to stick around."

This impressed Bart. Just the same it wasn't exactly, or entirely, what he wanted to hear, and what he needed to know. He thought about it for a bit and then he said, "You figure Mom would really have a fit if I shoved off?"

Alec stared at him. "Are you crazy?" he practically shouted. "She'd have a heart attack. She'd die!"

Bart thought a little more. "It might be better for you, though," he said then. "I mean, you could have everything your own way, and all."

Alec pushed both hands through his hair. "It's too late for that," he said, "let's face it. Anyway — things aren't really that bad at home. Mom's a terrific cook — you know? It could cost you a lot of money to eat the way she feeds us. And Pop — well, I guess you could meet

154

up with a lot worse types when you come right down to it. So why don't you stick around?" he said again.

Bart was with him. He was buying Alec's argument right down the line, especially about the food. And still there was something Alec hadn't said that Bart had to hear. They were almost at the town pier and if he was ever going to grapple with this problem, Bart decided he had to do it right now. He took a deep breath and got very casual and said, "But I guess you wouldn't die — I mean I guess you could stand it — if you never happened to see me again."

"What're you talking about?" Alec said gruffly. He sounded irritated and even downright annoyed. "After all, you're my brother, you know."

Bart relaxed all over. "Yeah, I guess that's right," he said.

"Besides," Alec added, "I might want to borrow your raft now and again."

Just then the boat bumped the town pier so hard that they both had to catch their balance. It gave Bart an excuse to laugh the way he wanted to, as if something were very funny, instead of just being happy, and great.